TURTLE TERROR

Charlotte Gibson Mysteries

Book 9

JASMINE WEBB

Chapter 1

I WAS LOCKED IN THE TRUNK OF A CAR, AND I knew if I panicked, I was dead. I mean, okay, even if I didn't panic, there was a good chance I was dead anyway. But keeping a cool head gave me the best chance of survival.

I grimaced as I tried to focus. My whole body was sore. That was an aftereffect of the Taser, though I was actually kind of getting used to it by now. My head hurt. When the two men had shoved me into the trunk, they'd hit my head on the frame, and now it felt like someone had stabbed a screwdriver directly between my eyes.

My mouth, hands, and feet were duct-taped. I struggled against the tape that bound my hands behind my back, but it was no use. Under me, the floor of the car began to vibrate; the engine was running. They were driving me somewhere.

I felt around for my phone. Nothing. That wasn't exactly a surprise; they weren't dumb enough to let me keep it. That would have been all too easy. So instead, I closed my eyes, ignored the pounding in my head, and focused on the road.

The car turned right. That meant we were back on the highway. We stopped, the engine idling for a few seconds. Then another right. I knew where we were. We were headed down the highway toward Kihei. Sure enough, the car began to speed up. I had about twenty minutes to find a way out of here before I was dead.

The Ham brothers had come for me. And they'd gotten me.

I struggled to find something in this trunk that could help me. Anything. But no, these guys weren't idiots. I was sure I wasn't the first person who had taken a trip in the trunk of the Ham brother's vehicle. These weren't some amateurs, committing their first kidnapping. They were professional bad guys. They wouldn't leave a spare knife just hanging around back here. Or even a tool kit hidden underneath the carpet that lined this rental car's floor.

You know what's worse than being kidnapped? Being kidnapped and knowing there's nothing you can do about it. Lying in the trunk of a car for twenty minutes, racing toward Kihei, knowing that you can't escape. You can't do anything. Or at least, that was the worst part for me. I wasn't about to give them the satisfaction of screaming and punching. Why would I? I needed that energy for when they got me out of here. So I lay there, every second feeling like an hour, knowing that we were getting closer and closer to a death that would not be quick and painless.

Even the route we were taking made that obvious. If we'd been headed Upcountry, I could have let myself believe that they were just going to pull me out of the trunk, shoot me, and dump my body along the myriad of rural roads on that part of the island. But no. Kihei was much more populated than that, which meant they had a plan. The odds were good they were planning on taking their time with me. And there was nothing I could do about it.

Eventually I gave up, lying on the floor of the trunk and stewing. When I got out of here, I would kick some ass. I wasn't the same woman I was back in Seattle. They couldn't know that. I'd found myself. Found a life. And I was going to fight like hell to keep it, no matter what it took.

Jake was in the hospital. Zoe, Dot, Rosie—no one would even know I was missing. I had told Jake I was going home. It would be hours before anyone would even know to raise the alarm, and by then, I'd probably be fish food if I didn't do something.

After what felt like an eternity, the car slowed. Made a right. We'd just turned off the highway. I knew we were in Kihei somewhere.

The car drove through the local streets, making a turn here and there. I wasn't one hundred percent sure, but I had a sneaking suspicion we were in the area near the Safeway.

Then the car slowed to a stop, and all my senses were on high alert. I heard a creak. Maybe a gate? That would make sense. This group would want privacy while they tortured me and then chopped my body up into little pieces.

I steadied myself as I waited for the trunk to open. When it did, I struck. The trunk clicked, a bit of light streamed through a slit, and as soon as it got larger, I kicked out at one of the men with my bound feet. I nailed him in the stomach, and he let out a gasp, stumbling backward as he clutched his abdomen.

The other guy growled and reached forward. He grabbed me by the hair, holding the Taser in front of me. "Bitch, give me another excuse to use this."

The first man coughed deeply a couple of times. "Use it. She deserves it, fucking bitch. She's dead once Braden gets here, anyway."

"He said not to hurt her until then," the other man snapped. He yanked my hair, and I yelped through the duct tape as he dragged me out of the

4

trunk. The two men grabbed me, one hooking his hands under my arms and the other taking hold of my feet.

I blinked rapidly, letting my eyes adjust to the light. We were in a garage. Going by the bare minimum of items, and the weathered, light blue sign on the wall announcing in a cutesy script, "if you're not barefoot, you're overdressed", I had a feeling this was an Airbnb or other vacation rental. Did the product description offer "the perfect secluded spot to commit your revenge kidnapping and murder," I wondered?

I was plonked unceremoniously down on the concrete floor, wincing as my collarbone hit it hard, and watched as one of the men pulled the car back out into the driveway. I guessed they needed more space to torture me. While the first man drove, I got a better look at my other captor.

He was the one I'd kicked in the stomach. A shade over six feet tall, his black hair was slicked back, which made him resemble a wannabe Don Draper but really just emphasized the obvious fact that his hairline was receding faster than the glaciers in Alaska. He wore jeans and a long-sleeved plaid shirt. Those clothes were normal wear in Seattle, but they stuck out like a sore thumb here on the island. How this guy wasn't sweating out of every pore was beyond me.

As soon as the car pulled out of the driveway,

Knockoff Don Draper headed to the corner and unfolded a large tarp on the floor. Great. Tarps were always a good sign when you'd just been kidnapped. Not.

He then placed a simple wooden chair on top of it and heaved me to my feet. "Jesus Christ, how much do you eat?" he muttered as he hoisted me up.

I rolled my eyes as he dragged me to the chair and plopped me down on it, just as his buddy returned and closed the garage door behind him. The car outside was a late-model white Toyota, I noted. As the door rolled down, I couldn't help but think that if I didn't act fast, that was going to be the last view of the outside world I would ever have.

The second man was a bit shorter than his friend, probably about five foot eight. He looked like the kind of guy who had an annoying podcast. Totally bald, with small, beady dark-brown eyes, he looked like a snowman built in reverse. His upper body was completely jacked, but his legs were like twigs. He didn't walk around. He strutted, but he did so the way men did when they tried to look confident but ended up looking like they were doing an exaggerated runway walk. It was very obviously hiding some deep-set insecurities.

I kept a mental note of that.

Reverse Snowman pulled out the Taser and

held it in front of my face. "If we take this duct tape off, you're not going to scream, right? Or you're going to get another taste of this bad boy."

I nodded, and Reverse Snowman yanked the duct tape from my mouth. The sting caused my eyes to water. I blinked back the tears and glared at them both. "I'm going to enjoy ruining your lives."

Knockoff Don Draper laughed. "Sure, babe. Whatever you say."

He grabbed a roll of duct tape from the lone shelf in this garage and approached me. He wrapped the tape around my waist, tying me to the chair.

Meanwhile, Reverse Snowman headed to a mini fridge in the corner and grabbed two beers. He popped the tops and handed one of them to Knockoff Don Draper, and the two men drank while their eyes bored into me. This wasn't the first time they had done this, and they were enjoying the moment. They wanted to watch me squirm. Well, it wasn't going to happen.

I slouched in the chair as much as I could, doing my best to look bored.

Reverse Snowman chugged most of his drink, then the phone in his pocket binged. He finished his beer then pulled the phone from his pocket and read the screen.

A creepy smile spread across his face as he

looked at me. "Just got a message from the bosses. They've been held up; they're going to be a little late. They said we can do what we want to you, as long as we don't spoil the goods."

I knew what they were implying, but I refused to look intimidated, even though I was scared shitless. My heart pounded. How was I going to get out of here? I had no weapons. All I could do was try to talk my way out of this.

I looked down at Reverse Snowman's crotch and snorted. "Seriously? You think that's a threat? I know what you've got there, and I bet it'll look like a carrot that got pulled out of the ground two months early."

Anger flashed in Reverse Snowman's eyes. He grabbed the empty beer bottle, smashed the end of it against the wall, and rushed over toward me. Reverse Snowman held the broken bottle against my throat. The glass pressed against my skin, and I felt the warm flow of blood dripping down my neck.

Still, I refused to look scared.

"Do you want me to try with this instead?" he growled.

I looked Reverse Snowman in the eyes while I laughed. "I mean, at least then I'd actually feel something."

Reverse Snowman bared his teeth at me and

pressed the piece of glass deeper into my skin, but Knockoff Don Draper interrupted him.

"Sean," he snapped. "Don't. You kill her now, and we're as good as dead too. Braden's instructions were clear. Don't hurt her."

Sean's eyes bored into mine, anger roiling behind them. He ground his teeth together as he snarled. For a second, I thought his rage might take over and he was going to end my life right then and there, but finally, he pulled away. He threw the rest of the beer bottle on the floor and smashed it to pieces before storming back to the fridge and grabbing another beer.

"Fine, but she's not allowed to talk anymore," he snapped at me.

I grinned. "Hit a nerve, did I? I bet that's something you've never done to a woman."

Sean looked like he was going to attack me once more, but Knockoff Don Draper placed a hand on his chest and shoved him backwards with a warning glance. "No. Not right now." Then, he turned to me. "Shut the fuck up, will you?"

I shrugged, trying to look unfazed.

"I swear to God, Kyle, I'm going to fuck her up if they don't get here fast," Sean muttered to Knockoff Don Draper under his breath.

"Cool it, dude," Kyle replied through gritted teeth. "I don't want to deal with the fallout if you can't control yourself around some bitch for like half an hour."

"She said I had a small dick," Sean whined.

I began to laugh. "Oh no, did I hurt your feelings?" I said in an exaggerated toddler-like voice.

Before Kyle had a chance to stop him, Sean pushed past him, rushed over toward me grabbing the back of the chair I was tied on and shoving it sideways, tipping it over. "Shut the fuck up, bitch, or I'll give you something to cry about," he shouted as I slammed to the floor.

My head hit the concrete, and pain blasted through it. My vision moved in and out of focus, blackness moving into my periphery, but I maintained consciousness. And more importantly, my hands, tied at the wrists, were now able to touch the tarp. I reached out, patting with my hands until I found a large-ish piece of glass from the beer bottle Sean had smashed.

I carefully wrapped my hand around the glass piece as Kyle rushed over.

"Dude," he snapped as he pulled the chair back upright, the speed of it making my head spin. "Look what you've fucking done. There's glass in her face now."

"I don't give a shit," Sean replied, sulking in the corner as he took another swig of his beer. "She deserves it."

Kyle reached into the back of his waistband

and pulled out a gun, which he pointed at Sean. "If you can't handle yourself, then you're as much of a fucking liability as she is."

"Whoa, whoa," Sean said, holding up his hands. "What the fuck, dude?"

"I don't want to do this, but I will. Braden and Connor were clear. They're the ones who are going to be taking care of her. Got it?"

"Yeah, man. I got it. Put that away, Jesus."

Kyle shoved the gun back into the waistband of his jeans. While he and Sean argued, I began working the piece of glass against the duct tape wrapping my wrists together. My method wasn't without its issues. The glass cut through the tape, sure, but it also cut through my skin, and pain shot through the palm of my hand. The blood made it hard to get a good grip on the shard of glass, and I had to make sure to keep my fists closed, because if they saw the blood, they'd figure out quickly that I was cutting myself free.

After a minute or so, I finally felt the duct tape give. I'd cut all the way through. My hands were free, but I couldn't let my captors know that. After all, I was still tied to the chair at my waist, and my feet were duct-taped together too. I couldn't hack away at either of those without drawing attention to myself, so I just had to hold tight and wait for my opportunity.

As the minutes ticked away, Kyle and Sean

eventually settled into a frosty silence. They glance at me periodically, while I was well aware that it wouldn't be long before the Ham brothers showed up. And then, with four of them against me, I would be dead. No question. I had to do something before then.

"So, what's it like being the guy who wasn't trusted enough to carry a gun?" I asked Sean, flashing him a grin. My best bet was playing these two against each other.

"Shut the fuck up," Kyle snapped at me.

"I mean, I get it. You're obviously not the brains of this operation," I continued. "I wouldn't trust you with a gun either."

"Don't need one," Sean replied, baring his teeth at me. "I'm going to slit your throat when the Ham brothers are done with you. Even if you're already dead."

"Wow, nothing screams badass like mutilating an already-dead body," I replied casually. "Besides, I don't think you have the balls to do it. You haven't done anything here. Kyle's the one who had the Taser. And the gun. All you did was drink beer and threaten me then smash a bottle. That's why they don't trust you, isn't it? Because when it comes down to it, you're all talk."

"Don't listen to her," Kyle growled at Sean, whose hands had curled into fists so tight his knuckles turned white.

"How do you think this will end for you?" I asked Sean. "I mean, even though you're gangsters, this is still a business, right? The Peter principle applies. Have you risen to your highest level of competence and moved past that? Where you're now incompetent? I mean, from my point of view, that's obviously where you are. Kyle can see it, clear as day. He's going to tell the Ham brothers what went down here, because he knows you're putting his ass on the line, too. But there's one difference: in a regular job, you mess up enough times and you get fired. But here, what do you think's going to happen to you? You're going to end up with a bullet in your brain, aren't you? I mean, it's pretty obvious. Kyle just had to hold a gun to your head. Do you really think you've got a long-term future in this organization? And I'm guessing being a Ham brothers associate doesn't come with a pension plan."

"I'm a lieutenant, bitch," Sean snapped at me.

"I'll make sure they spell the title right on your gravestone, assuming they even find your body to bury."

"You're going to be dead long before I am," Sean replied, taking a couple of steps toward me.

He was two feet away when suddenly, the side door of the garage burst open. The three of us looked over. It was Jake.

Chapter 2

THIS WAS NOT EXACTLY A SCENE FROM A JAMES
Bond movie. Jake was still wearing his hospital
robe, but at some point, the tie had come open,
and he stood in front of us, with everything on
display. He held his gun in front of him, level,
ready to strike.

His appearance would have been really funny
if not for the whole life-or-death situation thing.

I took my chance. I stood up as much as I
could, still folded against the chair, and wrenched
my hands away from me. "An eye for a finger,
bitch," I shouted as I drove the shard of glass from
the beer bottle directly into Sean's eye.

He hadn't seen it coming; the glass slid into
him, and he screamed as blood poured from his
eye socket.

I squeezed my eyes shut as I shoved the shard

in, knowing this was my best chance at saving my life. Sean stumbled, yelling as he moved backward, right into Kyle, who was in the middle of drawing his weapon from his waistband.

"He's got a gun," I shouted in warning to Jake as I reached down and grabbed another shard of glass from the floor. Kyle's gun exploded, and then so did Jake's.

I hacked at the duct tape around my ankles, desperate to free myself. Next to me, a body slumped over. The sound of Sean's screams still pierced the air. When I was finally clear, I took in the scene.

Kyle had somehow shot Sean in the leg. Sean writhed on the floor, his focus split between the shard of glass that still stuck out of his eye and the blood seeping from the hole in his jeans, midway through the calf.

How the bullet had found those toothpick legs, I would never know, but I wasn't about to complain.

Kyle had dropped his gun on the floor and was clutching at his shoulder, blood seeping through his fingers. Jake had obviously hit his target.

"Get down," Jake ordered. "You're both under arrest."

"Under arrest? What the fuck?" Kyle managed to ask through gasps of pain. I had to admit, in his position, I probably would have asked the same thing. Not every cop on the island wandered around with no identification in an open hospital robe.

"Charlie, are you okay? Get out of here," Jake ordered, his gun still levelled at the two gangsters. I finally got a closer look at him. Sweat covered his brow. His face was a couple of shades too pale. He was breathing heavily. His hands were trembling slightly. I was sure he walked with a limp; he'd been shot in the ass under twelve hours ago.

And yet he was still here. He'd still found me. Still saved me.

"We're both leaving," I ordered. "The Ham brothers are coming. They're going to be here soon."

"I'm going to kill them," he snarled. "They can come here, and they're going to die."

"No," I said firmly. "Not right now. Let's get out of here. My hands are cut up to hell. You're, well, there's a whole laundry list of reasons why this is a bad idea for you right now. Let's go. We'll get them, but right now we need to leave."

My words seemed to make something click in Jake's brain. "Right," he said quickly. "Get outside."

I didn't need to be told twice. I raced out into the yard and out of the now-open gate. Queenie was parked at the front, with Zoe in the passenger seat. As soon as she saw me, her eyes widened. "Charlie!"

"Get in the back," I shouted to Jake, who was following me, his gun still trained on the house in case either of the gangsters decided to come out and start a firefight.

"I'm driving," he protested.

"My car, my rules. Besides, do you even realize your gown is wide open and you're putting on a show for the neighbors? Because I feel like if you don't, you're in no shape to drive."

Jake swore as he climbed into the back seat, wincing with pain as he grabbed the robe and covered himself once more. The car was already running, so I threw it into gear and peeled away from the curb. The tires squealed against the asphalt as we raced back toward the highway.

"Are you okay?" Zoe asked as I drove, looking me up and down with her keen doctor's eye. "Your hands. And face. You're bleeding."

"Nothing a few stitches won't fix," I said, keeping my eyes on the road. "Take care of Jake."

Zoe nodded and undid her seatbelt, climbing carefully into the back seat. "I told you this was a bad idea," she scolded Jake as he let out a cry of pain.

"Charlie's safe," he whispered. "It was all worth it."

"He's unconscious," Zoe said to me, her voice

serious but level. "We have to get him back to the hospital. He was in no shape to leave in the first place."

She climbed back into the passenger seat and did up her seatbelt while I glanced into the rearview mirror. Jake was lying on the seat, passed out.

"Is he going to be okay?" I asked, my voice trembling.

"He should be. But he never should have left."

Jake leaving had saved my life.

"What happened?" I asked.

"I was checking on him. A nurse in the parking lot found your keys and phone. She recognized them as yours. Apparently, you're the only person she knows whose keychain is a little iced coffee with "Menace to Society" printed on it."

I grinned. "I knew that would come in handy."

"Jake saw it and freaked out. We both knew something was wrong. So I took your phone, and I did what I figured you'd do. I called Dot and Rosie."

"Uh-oh," I said with a grimace. "Jake doesn't exactly know how, uh, good they are at things."

"I realized that when he asked me what I thought two old ladies could to do to help. Anyway, Dot got into the security camera footage, found the license plate of their rental, and hacked into the on-board emergency response system. She

told us they were taking you back to Kihei. Jake
started to get up, and I ordered him back into bed.
We had an argument. He said you were in danger
and that he wasn't about to let you die. And
frankly, that won me over. Because I wasn't about
to let you die either."

"So you drove over here?"

"I insisted on driving. Jake was in no condition
to drive. He'd just come out of surgery after
suffering a bullet wound. He should have been in
the hospital. He couldn't help you if he drove off
the road."

I glanced over at her and smiled. "I bet he
loved that."

"He tried to argue, but I had the keys. When I
told him he could get in or get left behind, he
jumped in. When we got there, he told me to stay
in the car and keep the engine running. That was
fine with me. I can patch people up once they've
hurt themselves, but I'm way worse at doing the
hurting."

"Good." Zoe was skilled at many things, but
jumping right into a dangerous crime scene with
gangsters who had just kidnapped her best friend
was not one of them. Luckily, she had a good head
on her shoulders and knew just that.

"You know the rest. He went in after you. He
was so scared, Charlie. So was I. Especially after I
heard the gunshots."

I gripped the wheel tightly, my knuckles turning white as we flew back up the highway. I was scared now. Jake had been shot, and now he lay unconscious in my back seat because he'd come all this way to save me, against medical advice.

Zoe's phone buzzed, and she answered, putting it on speaker. "We have her," she announced.

"Good," Rosie answered on the other end of the line. "Everyone is safe?"

"Yes. We're driving back to the hospital now. Jake shouldn't have left."

"He was always going to; he loves her," Dot said on Rosie's end of the line. "Charlie, are you there?"

"I am, and I hear I have you both to thank for saving my life. Again."

"I'm sorry I couldn't be there myself," Rosie said, her voice tinged with a soft note of regret, a rare emotion to hear from her. "I trusted Jake would get you out safely, and while he's now more aware of the role we play, I'm still not comfortable with him knowing precisely what my specific skills are. If I didn't truly believe the two of you would manage to get you out of this, however, I would have been there in a second."

"I know," I replied, my voice nearly cracking. I could hear in her voice just how much she cared for me. Just then, I realized how difficult that decision must have been for her and that she likely would have struggled with the need to keep her former identity secret for her own safety.

"What happened to the gang?" Dot asked. "Are they in custody?"

"No," I replied, drawn back to the reality of the present. I drummed my fingers on the steering wheel as I thought about the fact that the gangsters were still out there. Sure, one was probably missing an eye. But they weren't right here, in the car, at this moment. "They got away. Jake was in no condition to stop them."

"We'll find them," Dot said confidently.

"One of them is going to need medical attention. I stabbed him in the eye with a shard of glass."

"Good for you," Rosie replied immediately without skipping a beat. "If they do, they'll be easily tracked. That's not the sort of injury that's common on the island."

"I'll keep an eye out for names on the manifests of flights leaving the island," Dot said. "Did you see the Ham brothers?"

"No. They were running behind. That probably saved my life. It gave me a chance to get away. They're on the island, though. This is our chance. We have to get them."

"Do you know where you were being held?"

Dot asked. "I'm pretty sure I have the address from the GPS system, but a confirmation would be good."

I bit my lower lip. Would I be able to recognize it again? My adrenaline had been pumping as we left, so I completely forgot to grab an address.

"I do," Zoe replied before I had a chance to speak. "I'm texting you the address now."

"Excellent," Dot said. "I'll look into it and send the police over immediately. I'll be in touch. And Charlie?"

"Yeah?"

"I'm very happy you're okay."

Warmth radiated through me, and tears welled in my eyes. "Me too."

Zoe ended the call. "You hear that? Dot and Rosie are on it. It's going to be fine."

I couldn't help but glance into the back seat, where Jake was still passed out. "I hope so."

I PEELED INTO THE EMERGENCY DROP-OFF AREA AT the hospital and immediately called for help. "Police officer down," I shouted.

A nurse who had been standing outside, upon hearing those words and seeing Zoe, sprinted inside straightaway. Ten seconds later, a group emerged with a stretcher. Zoe took control.

"Patient is a thirty-two-year-old male, recovering from surgery to remove a gsw," she called out as the group worked together to move Jake from the Jeep and onto the stretcher.

The world faded away as I watched them work. Watched Jake. He'd literally escaped the hospital to come and save my life. And that was what he had done. I wasn't one hundred percent sure I would have gotten out of that garage alive if he hadn't burst in when he did.

Before I knew it, the hospital doors whooshed closed behind the medical professionals, and I was standing alone with Queenie. I looked down at myself. I was a mess. Covered in blood. Some of it mine. Some of it Sean's.

As the adrenaline faded, the reality set in. My face hurt like hell, especially when I moved. I still had small bits of glass embedded in my skin. My hands looked like I'd just lost a fifty-round slap-fight with a freshly-sharpened sword.

I parked Queenie in the lot and went to check myself in. I was safe. For now. But I knew it wouldn't last. The Ham brothers were on the island. They had come for me once. And they wouldn't be happy until I was dead.

I was just going to have to find them first.

Chapter 3

A FEW HOURS LATER, I WAS SITTING ON A HOSPITAL bed, and Zoe tutted as she looked at my wounds.

"This isn't my fault, for once," I complained. "You can't tut at me."

"I'm your doctor. I'm not tutting at you. I'm tutting at the injury."

"We both know you're tutting at me."

Zoe laughed. "You can request another physician, you know?"

"I don't want anyone else. Thanks for doing this. I know you're not actually supposed to be working right now."

"You're welcome. There's no one in the world whose face I'd rather be pulling glass from."

"What about Henry?" I asked in a singsongy voice.

Zoe shot me a look. "Do you really think

Henry is ever going to come in here with glass wedged into his face?"

"And yet you think it's normal for me."

"You're sitting here in front of me, aren't you? I swear, I'm practically your family doctor at this point, you've been here so often."

"Okay, I can't argue with that."

"I'm going to pick the glass out first. Then, we'll wash your face, and after that I'm going to do your hands. Got it?"

"Yes."

"I'm not going to inject anything here, but I am going to put a topical numbing lotion on your skin. It won't get rid of all the pain, but it will dull it somewhat."

I stared at the wall in front of me while Zoe carefully rubbed a cream on the side of my face. "How's Jake?" I asked.

"He's going to be fine. They took his vitals, got him hooked up on a new IV. It doesn't look like he tore anything during that incident. He needs to rest, not chase gangsters around the island. He's just been through surgery."

"If you really believed it was life-threatening, you would have stopped him," I pointed out.

"It was life-threatening. But then, you were in the same situation," Zoe said quietly as she picked up a pair of what looked like extra-long tweezers. "Now, sit still. I'm going to get these out."

I closed my eyes and tried not to think about what was happening as Zoe pulled piece after piece of glass out of my face. Every time she pulled on a shard, pressure and a bit of pain shot through me for a second. Then I'd hear the tinkle of glass against the bottom of the stainless-steel bowl beside her into which she dropped them.

After about six or seven times, Zoe said, "That's all for your face. Now, we need to clean this up. None of these wounds are big enough that you'll need stitches, but you're going to want to be careful while they heal. We want to avoid an infection."

She cleaned the wounds then started working on my hands. She sucked in air as soon as she saw them.

"That bad, huh?" I asked with a grimace.

"I'm not worried about the skin. That's fine. It will heal with time. But I'm just hoping none of these cuts were deep enough to hit tendons or ligaments that might mess with your ability to use your hands longer-term. Can you flex them?"

I squeezed my hands into a loose fist and stretched them back out a few times. "So far, so good."

"Excellent. That's a good sign. You'll want to keep an eye on it, though."

"I will. Given that the alternative was a painful death, I'll take a bum hand."

Zoe's mouth pressed into a hard line. "Me too."

The cuts on my hand were larger and deeper than the ones on my face. This time, she injected a painkiller and gave me nine stitches across both hands.

"I want to make you promise me to take it easy for a little while, but we both know you'd be lying," Zoe said quietly when she had finished. My hands looked like they belonged to Frankenstein's monster. But I was here. I wasn't dead.

"Yeah," I admitted. "I can't. Not until they're in jail. They tried to kill me."

"Take care of yourself, Charlie. I know you're going to get revenge. Hell, I want you to get it. I want them out of your life forever. But I want you in mine forever too."

"I'll do my best," I said with a smile as I headed back out into the hallway. Instead of turning to the exit, I made my way to the surgery ward, where Jake was back in his bed, still unconscious.

I leaned against the doorway and watched the slow up-and-down movement of his chest. Jake had saved my life tonight. If it weren't for him, who knew what would have happened?

"You should go home," Zoe said quietly behind me.

I shook my head. "No. I'm not leaving him."

"Okay. Let me get you a blanket and pillow, at least."

I walked into the room carefully, as if my mere presence could put Jake in more danger. After I took a seat in the chair next to him, Zoe returned a minute later with a warm blanket and a pillow, and I sat there, staring at him, wondering what was going to happen next.

I MUST HAVE FALLEN ASLEEP AT SOME POINT, because when I woke up the next morning, Jake was awake, looking over at me with an amused smile.

"You snore when you sleep upright," he said.

I stuck my tongue out at him. "Careful. I'll put you in the hospital if you keep lying like that."

Jake barked out a laugh then grimaced. "Ugh. Laughing was a mistake. I can't do that yet."

"How are you feeling?" I asked, scooching my chair closer to the edge of the bed.

"Like I got hit by a truck."

"You're going to be here for a few days." Then, I lowered my voice. "Thanks for saving my life."

Jake's eyes met mine, and the corners of his mouth curved upward. "I don't know. It looked like you had it pretty well handled."

"A cop going full frontal while aiming a gun at them is always a good distraction, though," I replied with a chuckle.

"Shit. I thought I dreamt that part in a hazy morphine dream."

"Nope. There are two members of the Ham gang out there who saw your whole, well, salami."

"I told you not to make me laugh," Jake complained, wincing.

"Can't help it. I'm just too funny. But seriously, I'm glad you're okay. You passed out in the car on the way back. I told you it was a better idea to let me drive."

"You were right," he admitted. "I guess I wasn't quite ready to leave the hospital. Zoe tried to stop me, but I... I couldn't... I couldn't let you."

"I know," I said softly, squeezing his hand. "And I'm glad you did."

We sat in silence for a minute, neither one of us wanting to think about what would have happened in Jake hadn't burst in at that exact moment.

"Have you heard anything? Have they been caught?"

"I don't know," I admitted. "Zoe grabbed the address where we were and sent it to Dot and Rosie. They were going to call the police."

"Speaking of, I knew Dot and Rosie did more than they always implied."

I gave Jake a wry smile. "Everyone tends to underestimate them because of their age."

"No kidding. Well, I won't make that mistake again. I half expected them both to show up at the house in a tank."

"Maybe if you hadn't been on your way," I said, cracking a smile.

"They wouldn't even tell me the whole story. I know there's more to them than they showed me, and they did things I couldn't believe. The speed at which they tracked down those men was incredible."

"Are you going to dig into them?" I asked.

"No. They obviously trusted me enough to show me what they were willing to do to save your life, and I respect that. I'm not going to take advantage. But damn. If one of them has super-human powers, you have to tell me. I need to be able to tell Childhood Jake if the X-Men are real."

I laughed. "Okay, they're not *that* good, although it does feel that way sometimes."

"You should go home, Charlie. Get some real rest. I'll be fine here. Find out what happened. And stay safe, okay? If they're not caught, go stay with Carmen."

I scrunched up my face. "I think I'll take my

chances with the gang before I live with my mom again."

"I'm serious. They're bad news."

"I'll be safe. I promise. You're sure you're good here?"

"I am. They're taking good care of me."

"I can't believe you got shot in the butt and I barely got to make fun of it before something else happened," I said. Then I leaned over and planted a kiss on Jake's lips.

"Oh, I'm sure I'm never going to hear the end of it regardless," he replied, his eyes twinkling as I pulled away.

I walked toward the door and turned to look at Jake before I left.

"Hey Jake?"

"Yeah?"

"I… I love you," I said, tripping over the first word.

"I love you too," he replied, the corners of his eyes crinkling as a smile spread across his face.

WITH THE ADRENALINE HAVING WELL AND TRULY worn off, I realized just how much the previous night's events had affected my body. I limped out of the hospital like I'd just gone six rounds toe-to-toe with Mike Tyson. My left hip was in agony with every step. My knees felt like someone had replaced their cartilage with gravel. Random muscles in my back and shoulder ached.

I reached Queenie and flopped into the driver's seat, wincing with pain. Once I'd pulled out my phone, I dialed Dot's number.

"Hey," I said when she answered.

"How are you doing?"

"Cuts and bruises. A few stitches. Mostly okay. I spent the night at the hospital, making sure Jake was okay. He's going to recover, but it'll take some time."

"I'm glad to hear it. Come on over. I'll show you what we have."

"Have the men been arrested?"

"No," Dot said, her disappointment obvious in her voice. "I called the police as soon as we ended our call last night. They arrived at the home, but by the time they'd gotten there, everyone had cleared out. They're going to get in contact with Airbnb to try to find the contact info for the men, but we both know they're not going to get anywhere."

"No. They were obviously careful. And I don't think they're going to go to the hospital, either, despite one-eyed Sean needing medical attention."

"They won't risk it. Not on the island. They know the police are going to be after them. That's why they cleared out of the home so quickly.

Either he's going to die of a raging infection in the near future, or they're going to try to get him off the island, or they're going to try to find someone who can take care of him under the table."

I blew out a puff of air as I started the car and began driving out of the parking lot. "If he leaves Maui, then that's a double-edged sword. He'd be away from me, but we wouldn't be able to catch him."

"Right. We need to track him down, either way. And the others."

"They're going to come after me again. We know it. This only ends one way."

"Yes. Let's try to get to them before they leave the island."

"I'll be there soon."

I ended the call and focused on the drive over to Dot's place.

Chapter 4

IT WAS NEARLY TEN O'CLOCK IN THE MORNING when I pulled into a visitor's parking spot at Dot's complex. After walking up to it, I knocked on her door and was immediately ushered in by Rosie, who took me in a warm and unexpected hug.

"Oh," I said in shock, returning it.

"I'm glad you're all right," she said. "This was your first time being kidnapped by hardened criminals, right?"

"I like how we now have to specify how experienced my kidnappers are," I replied. "But yes. The others were amateurs."

"This group is anything but," Dot said from her spot at the computer, where she was typing away at the keyboard. "It's no wonder they've gotten away with what they have for so long in the Seattle area. This isn't twenty-year-olds trying to

cosplay the Bloods and the Crips. They're struc-
tured well, they keep under the radar, and they
know when to pack it in. Like last night. They left
the Airbnb almost immediately. They wiped it
down and everything. The police have nothing.
I'm running all of their credit cards, but nothing is
popping up. Wherever they're staying now, they're
not using credit cards in their names to do it. They
know better than that, and it's a rare skill in this
day and age."

"They'll have fake IDs," Rosie pointed out.
"And possibly cards in those names as well. We
won't be able to track them that way."

"We could try the rental car," Dot said,
suddenly speeding up her tapping on the
keyboard. "If they used a fake name to rent it,
they may have used that same false identity to find
somewhere else to stay on the island. Give me a
bit."

While Dot did that, Rosie took a careful look
at my injuries. "You've been patched up pretty
well," she said approvingly. "You do have a few
bruises, though."

"You should see the other guy."

I settled myself on the couch with a groan as
Dot worked. Rosie grabbed me a glass of water,
which I drank gratefully, carefully holding the glass
with my fingertips to avoid aggravating the stitches
on my hands. It would be at least a few days

before I began to feel remotely normal again, I was sure.

"There's something going on outside," Rosie noted as she walked past the patio window. "The police are here."

"Quick, hide the computers," I joked quickly.

Dot snorted. "Please. Like they could get access to my files. Everything here is booby trapped. If they try to physically move any of my devices, it all gets wiped."

"There's a few of them, too," Rosie said, frowning as she looked down at the parking lot below. "I wonder what's happening."

"This isn't normally a high-crime complex," Dot pointed out. "Mostly retirees. Albert down the hall insists on having every single conversation on speakerphone when he's out in public, which *should* be illegal, and he deserves to go to jail for it, but the law has yet to catch up with my correct opinion."

"I agree with you, for what it's worth," I said.

"Thank you."

Dot continued typing away, while Rosie stood near the patio window, peering carefully through a small gap in the drapes every couple of minutes.

After about twenty minutes, I told her, "You look like a stalker. Or an old lady with nothing to do but to spy on the neighbors."

"They still haven't left," Rosie replied. "Whatever the police are here about, it's big. I'm going to see if I can find out who's involved. Stay here."

"You don't have to tell me twice," I replied as I watched Rosie. She slipped on her shoes and left.

"I'm in," Dot announced about a minute later. "I've got the rental car company records. Now we just need to match the license plate number to a name."

"I imagine that'll take you all of thirty seconds."

"Even less, I've already got it." She turned to me and grinned. "Evan Walsh. That's the name one of them was using. Come here. Does he look familiar?"

I groaned as I struggled to get to my feet and shuffled over to Dot. Despite being the youngest person here by decades, I somehow felt like the oldest.

On the screen was a picture of an Ohio driver's license. The photograph staring out at me showed Kyle, with his slicked-back hair and beady, deep-set eyes. The slight fisheye lens made his cheeks puff out more than they had in person, giving him an even creepier vibe than normal. My heart lurched, the memory of his attempting to murder me rushing back at the sight of him.

"That's Kyle. I don't have a last name. One of the men who was holding me."

"Got it. At least now we have his alias. Evan

Walsh. We can track him. Is he the guy you turned into a pirate?"

"Nope. That was Sean."

"Too bad. That might have made him easier to find if he checked into any hospitals. All the same, let me run this ID. See if we can get a location on him. They might have used his name to get a hotel room or another vacation rental."

As I settled back down on the couch, Rosie entered the apartment once more.

"There's been a murder," she announced.

I immediately sat upright. "What? Here? In this complex?"

"Please tell me someone finally got tired of Albert and did him in," Dot muttered.

"No, it was out on the water. Not even on Maui, in fact. The son of a woman down the hall. He worked as a captain for one of the tour operators that takes groups out snorkeling. He dropped the whole group off in Lanai, and when they got back onto the boat, they found his body."

Dot snapped around in her chair and faced Rosie, suddenly interested. "Which woman? Whose son?"

"Four doors down from here, across the hall. Apartment sixteen."

Dot inhaled sharply. "Oh no. That's Matthew Hogan. His mother is Gail. What a tragedy."

"You know him?" I asked.

Dot nodded. "Yes. I always liked him. Gail was a single mother; her husband left when Matthew was two. She raised him in that apartment. He was a good kid. Always polite without being patronizing. I was the one who suggested he go into boating. He was always in the water, that child. I thought it would be perfect for him. Do you know what happened?"

Rosie shook her head. "No more than what I've just told you."

"Who on earth could have killed him?" Dot muttered to herself. "He was such a kind young man."

"You know, I don't have any cases now that we solved the bombing," I pointed out. "And while we're trying to find the Ham brothers, having something to distract me from the fact that I'm being hunted by gangsters and my boyfriend is in the hospital could be good."

"I'm happy to help you," Rosie said. "And to act as your bodyguard. I don't think you should wander around the island on your own at the moment."

I opened my mouth to protest, but before I had a chance to say anything, Rosie held up a hand. "Don't. You know I'm right. They attacked you out of nowhere yesterday. You didn't see it coming, and because of it, you nearly died. Do you really think they would have gotten you into that trunk if I was there?"

I paused. Rosie was right. And this was about more than just me now. Rosie and Dot had revealed themselves partially to Jake so they could find me. Jake had risked his life, leaving the hospital immediately after surgery to save me, and Zoe had gone alone with him, knowing how much danger I was in. I wasn't just putting myself in harm's way anymore. I was opening the people I loved up to peril as well. So as much as I hated to admit it, it wasn't just about me.

"Okay," I said. "You can be my associate. I'll offer to help, and we'll see what happens."

"Tell her I sent you," Dot ordered, her eyes back on the screen. "Gail is a wonderful woman. She's going to be broken up, but she trusts me. If you tell her I think this is a good idea, she'll see sense."

Rosie and I walked down the hall. I paused in front of the door to apartment sixteen. Taking a deep breath, I closed my eyes. I hated this part of the job. I was about to intrude on someone in the worst moment of her life, in the hopes that I might be able to offer her some justice at some point in the future. But that didn't mean this conversation wouldn't suck.

When I knocked, I heard shuffling on the

other side of the door. A few seconds later, it opened, and I stood facing Gail Hogan.

Gail was all circles. A round face. Enormous blue eyes, red-rimmed from crying. Plump lips and curly chestnut hair flecked with grey that surrounded her head like a halo. She wore a form-fitting wrap dress that accentuated her curves, and she looked at us with a mixture of hope and despair.

As if she wished we would take back the news that she'd just received but knowing it wasn't going to happen all the same.

"Gail Hogan, I'm Charlie Gibson," I told her. In my experience, getting straight to the point was the kindest thing one could do for a person in this situation. "I'm friends with Dot, down the hall. She sent me here to speak with you. I'm a private investigator, and I heard about your son. I'm so sorry for your loss."

"Thank you," Gail replied in a shaky voice, her hand reaching out automatically to the door-frame, which she clutched. "Dot has told me about you. You're her friend."

"I am, and I find killers. The Maui Police do their best, but Dot liked your son. She likes you. She thinks you both deserve justice, so if you're willing to have me help, I would like to find the person who did this to Matthew."

Gail nodded, as if she didn't trust herself to

speak, and stepped to the side to let Rosie and me enter. "The police just left. Please, come in."

"I'm very sorry," Rosie said quietly.

"I've seen you with Dot. You're here a lot," Gail told her.

"Yes. I'm Rosie. It's very nice to meet you."

"Any friend of Dot's is a friend of mine," Gail said, placing a hand on Rosie's forearm and squeezing it slightly. She led us through the apartment, which was laid out identically to Dot's.

In the living room, I took a seat on the well-worn, upholstered brown couch while Gail pottered around in the kitchen.

"Would either of you like anything?" she asked.

"No, thank you," we replied in unison.

Gail reappeared with a plate of shortbread cookies topped with flecks of coconut, which she placed on the small coffee table between Rosie and me. She took a spot in an armchair across from us and immediately began playing with a loose thread in the arm.

"You're saying you can find out who killed my son?" Gail asked while I took a cookie from the plate and nibbled the end. My stomach began to rumble at the promise of food; I couldn't remember the last time I'd eaten.

"We can do our best to try," I replied. "We have a lot of experience in solving murders."

Gail nodded. "I remember you. You're the one who solved that whole thing with Marion Hennessey."

"That was me."

"Then please, I ask you, do what you can for Matt. He was my sweet boy. An innocent angel. He had never done anything bad in his life, and I can't imagine who would have wanted to kill him."

Gail struggled over the penultimate word, still not quite ready to speak the reality aloud.

"I don't have a lot of money, but whatever I do have…"

I waved a hand. "Don't worry about that. Consider it a favor from Dot. I promise, we will do everything we can to find his murderer. Matt was killed at work?"

"That's what the police told me."

"Who did he work for?"

"A company called Zodiac Cruises. They take tourists on snorkeling trips around the island. They leave from Maalea Harbor. That's what Matt was doing yesterday. The police said they found him on the boat when they came back from their excursion."

"Did they tell you how he died?" I asked quietly.

Gail's voice was nearly inaudible. "He was stabbed. Someone stabbed my boy."

"And you can't think of anyone who would have done this to him? He had no enemies?"

Gail shook her head so hard it looked like a blur. "No. No. Absolutely not. My Matt was a good boy. Did you know he still came over for dinner every Sunday night? Most men his age, they're trying to stay away from their mothers. They want their own lives, pretending they don't need us anymore. But Matt knew what I'd gone through to raise him. He appreciated the sacrifices I made, and he always told me he was going to take care of me. Forever. That's the kind of man Matt was."

"Did he have a girlfriend?" Rosie asked.

"Yes. Oh, how am I going to tell Andi? They've been dating for about three months. I know, that's not very long these days, but I think Matt was truly beginning to fall in love with her. He didn't want to scare her off by introducing us too quickly, but he told me all about her. He met her at work. That means she would know, wouldn't she?" Gail's eyes darted between Rosie and me, as if begging one of us to tell her the answer.

"I think it's likely," I replied.

"I do hope she's doing all right. Poor Andi."

"And their relationship was fine?" I asked.

"It was. At least, Matt never mentioned anything."

"Men don't always tell their mothers every-thing," Rosie suggested gently.

"My Matt did," Gail said, sticking her chin out slightly. This was a point of pride for her. "He knew. I always told him, ever since he was a baby, that if anything was going on, I would never judge him. I would only help him. And he always came to me. Every time he had a problem, big or small. He kept no secrets from me."

"Can you think of anyone else who might have known what was going in his life?" I asked, then added quickly, "Not that he wouldn't tell you about anything. We just want to get as many facts and perspectives as possible."

"His best friend, Konane. He works in construction. I don't know how to get in touch with him, but Matt said he'd been working on building a house in Wailea, up behind the high-way. Andi might know. His number would be in his phone, if the police give it back to me."

"Okay, thank you," I said. "If there's anything else you can think of, please let Dot know."

"I will. And thank her from me, will you? The police are all right, but I want Matt's killer found. He deserves justice. They took my baby, and they deserve to go to jail."

"I'll do my best," I said, offering Gail a sympa-thetic smile as Rosie and I stood and headed back to the door.

As I said goodbye to Gail, I could see the hope in her eyes. I was going to do everything I could to get justice for her son. As soon as the door closed behind us, there came a wail from the other side, and my heart broke for the mother behind it.

Chapter 5

ROSIE AND I RETURNED TO DOT'S APARTMENT. As soon as we entered, Dot spun around in her chair, frowning. "The fake identity of Evan Walsh hasn't been used since he rented the car. No hotel bookings. No Airbnb. He hasn't even as much as bought McDonald's with the credit card in that name."

I groaned. "So we're nowhere."

"I'll continue digging and keep an eye on all the flight manifests, but we do likely need them to resurface before we have a lead on where they are," Dot admitted. "What about Gail? What did you find out from her? I'll go and see her in a little while, offer my condolences, but I want to give her some time to process, first."

"Matt was murdered," I confirmed. "Stabbed on the boat he was on."

JASMINE WEBB

"On the bright side, that limits the potential suspect pool," Rosie pointed out. "We'll get the details from the company, but if the boat was at a snorkeling spot, it's likely that the number of people who could have killed him is low. It had to be someone who was on that ship, or a nearby one."

"How well did you know Matt as an adult?" I asked Dot.

"Not very," she confessed with a small shrug. "Once he moved out, I saw him very rarely. But every time I did, he was always very nice. A polite young man. I wouldn't have blamed him for ignoring the other people in the building he no longer connected to, but he didn't. He was always willing to stop and chat if he saw me."

"But you don't know who might have wanted to kill him?"

"No, we certainly weren't that close."

"Okay. I'm going to check out his social media and stuff. I have to go home. Plus, I'm exhausted. Every bone in my body hurts. And I'm pretty sure Coco will have peed on the floor by now."

I felt a twinge of guilt at having left my poor dog alone overnight.

"I'm coming with you," Rosie said.

"No, it's fine. Seriously. I'm going to be okay. How are they going to know I was here, anyway?"

50

"You drive what is possibly the most recognizable car on this island. It's not going to be difficult for them to determine you're at home if your bright blue Jeep is parked in your spot."

I frowned. "Fine. Swap cars with me for a bit?"

Rosie pursed her lips, considering it. Eventually, she said, "Fine. And make sure to park in the visitors' spots only. And be careful when you're getting in and out. You don't want to be jumped again. Watch the upholstery, too. I just had it cleaned."

"I'll be careful. I promise."

"You need to be armed at all times too. Carry a small knife with you, at the very least. Here."

Rosie walked swiftly to the stand at the entryway near the door. Reaching into her purse, which sat on top, she pulled out a couple of items and handed them to me. "This one is Mace. I don't think I have to tell you not to point it at your own face before you press down on the trigger, but you've been Tasered more times than Elizabeth Taylor was married, so you never can be too careful."

"Almost none of those were my fault," I protested.

"'Almost' being the key to that sentence," Rosie replied, shooting me a pointed look as she firmly placed the bottle of Mace in my hand. It reminded me of a bottle of men's deodorant spray. Small, with a trigger on the top.

"Isn't there supposed to be like, one of those rings that you pull out of this to stop you from accidentally Macing people?" I asked, looking at the bottle carefully.

"Normally, yes. But I find them to be a waste of time. If you truly need to use the Mace, you want it to be available immediately. Besides, since I am a responsible adult, even without the safety pin inserted, I have yet to accidentally use this on anybody."

"Good to know."

"And take this knife," Rosie ordered, placing a small pocket knife next to the Mace in my palm. The weapon was plain, black, only a few inches long when folded, with a glossy black handle. "Keep it on you at all times. Practice opening and closing it. You need to be able to do it within a second—and one-handed."

"Okay. I will, I promise."

"Good. And if you see anyone or anything suspicious, call me immediately. I will be over there straightaway."

The seriousness with which Rosie treated the situation told me both how much she cared and how much she knew these people were bad news.

She was experienced. If Rosie was worried, then I knew I had to be careful.

"I'm not going to get caught unawares twice," I said. "Believe me."

Satisfied, Rosie nodded. "All right. Take my car. We'll be in touch. And text me when you're safely inside your apartment."

"I'll let you know if these guys pop back up onto the radar," Dot added. "And I'm going to try to track down their other identities. Don't worry, Charlie. We'll get them."

I knew if anybody could get this done, it was Dot.

I SAID GOODBYE TO DOT AND ROSIE AND WENT downstairs. In the parking lot, I climbed into Rosie's SUV instead of Queenie. It was so... reasonable. Rosie had even gotten the interior re-upholstered to hide the bullet marks after a killer had shot at us inside the vehicle. I would have totally kept them for the vibes.

As I was pulling into my complex, Mom called. I mashed the speakerphone button as I began to park.

"Hi, Charlie. Listen, I was talking to Lucas, and we were wondering if you'd like to come have dinner with us at some point, maybe in a couple of days. He really wants to meet you."

Immediately, I was six years old again, transported back to a time and place in which I didn't know what was going on, in which I was alone, drifting, unmoored. Not knowing how to handle social situations.

"Can Zoe come?" I found myself answering. Yup, that was me, at six years old again. Always wanting Zoe there with me, because she was my best friend.

The silence on the other end of the line for a couple of seconds betrayed Mom's surprise, but she recovered quickly. "Yes, of course. It's been much too long since I've seen Zoe. And it might be nice to do it in more of a group setting. She's more than welcome. And so is her boyfriend. What was his name? Henry?"

"That's right," I said, smiling to myself. I knew Mom was well aware of Henry's name. The only thing in the world Mom wanted to see more than me getting married and having kids was to see Zoe getting married and having kids. Every time I spoke to her, she asked about Zoe and Henry.

"Well, by all means, yes. Have them come too. After all, you and Zoe are closer than sisters."

"Thanks, Mom. I appreciate that."

"Let me know what times work for you. We're pretty open most evenings."

"I will. Thanks."

I walked upstairs to find a note from Henry, letting me know that Zoe messaged him about what had happened and that he'd come over, given Coco breakfast, and let her out to do her business.

My little dachshund-golden retriever mix, however, immediately set about convincing me that in fact, Henry was lying, and that while sure, she'd gone outside, she hadn't been fed in days. Maybe even weeks. It had been so long that she couldn't remember and was on the brink of starvation.

"See that? Right there? It says Henry fed you," I explained, picking up the note, placing it in front of her long face, and pointing out the part in which Henry said he gave her food.

Coco responded by biting the edge of the note and beginning to chew.

Dogs.

"Okay, you're starving. I guess you do deserve a treat," I conceded. I headed to the cupboard and gave her a piece of dried liver. Then I looked around and took a deep breath as I stood in my home. My whole body was still sore. The anesthetic in my hands was wearing off, and I felt like I was wearing a pair of leather gloves that was about three sizes too small. But sitting here and wondering what I could do to catch the gangsters who had just tried to kill me wouldn't do anything.

"Come on, Coco," I announced to my dog. "We're going to go on a trip to Grandma's for a few days. How does that sound?"

Coco let out a yip and wagged her tail, but since she was gazing firmly at the drawer from which the treats had magically appeared, I knew her excitement had nothing to do with going to my mom's.

I got all her things ready and packed her back up in Rosie's car. Mom wasn't home, so I let myself in, let Coco out, and left Mom a note letting her know why she suddenly had custody of my dog for a few days. Well, okay, I lied in the note. Mom would have freaked out if she knew how much danger I was in.

With Coco taken care of, I loaded myself back into Rosie's SUV and drove out to the Zodiac Cruises headquarters. Maalea was a small area on the corner where South Maui met West Maui. Calling it a neighborhood would have been overstating it. The whole area consisted of about three roads. There was a harbor, a handful of businesses, and a few condo buildings. The Maui Aquarium was the primary tourist center in this part of town.

I parked in the harbor and walked back across

the street to the low-rise building that housed most of the local businesses. Zodiac Cruises had a stenciled sign on the door announcing the name of the business. A circular logo underneath it displayed each of the twelve signs of the zodiac.

I was worried the door might be locked, since all the employees had gone home from the day, but when I tried the door, I found it open. The inside looked as I expected. On the right-hand side was a tall desk, above which was a red sign printed with white letters that read "Check in here!" in a marine-style font, surrounded by prints of *honu*, dolphins, and a variety of fish.

The left wall was decorated with printed pictures of underwater scenes, taken by a local photographer and offered for sale to any tourists who weren't pleased with what their GoPro had come up with on their tours.

Deeper in the center of the store was a small merchandise section. Swimsuits, flip-flops, rash guards, snorkels, and more were available for purchase.

In front of the desk stood two police officers. They were speaking to a woman in her twenties, her blond hair in a bob that hung just above her shoulders. She had obviously been crying; her eyes were puffy and bloodshot, but neither officer seemed to care.

As soon as I entered, one of them turned around. "This business is closed for today," he told me. Built like a linebacker but standing only about five foot five, this guy was the closest thing to a human square I'd ever seen.

"I'm not here to shop, I'm here to see Andi," I replied curtly.

"She's out the back," the blond woman said before the police had a chance to interrupt.

"Thanks," I said, flashing her a sad smile. The woman acknowledged me with a barely visible nod. Her gaze went blank once more as she stared ahead.

"You can't go back there," the square cop said, shaking his head. "This is a crime scene."

"My understanding is that the boat is a crime scene."

The other officer, a woman with a brown pixie cut, narrowed her eyes at me. "How do you know what's happened?"

"I've been hired by the family to find out who did this. I'm Charlie Gibson, private investigator. And I'm going to speak to Andi."

"Now you just hold on there," the square officer said. "You can't just go back there and speak to her."

"I'd love to hear what law I'm breaking," I replied as I continued walking toward the back of the store. "Since she was on the boat with

Matthew, presumably you've already taken her statement. And if you haven't, well, you're not very good at this, are you?"

Both cops glared at me, but neither spoke. Obviously, they weren't the sharpest tools in the shed. So, I turned around and headed to the door marked Staff Only. That was easy.

I pushed through the door and found myself in a small office. A large desk and plenty of cabinets filled the space, and against the far wall, a whiteboard listed boats, crews, schedules, and suggested itineraries. Four people milled around the room. One man was sitting in the office chair, slowly spinning it from side to side as he stared at the floor.

Two women comforted each other, leaning against one another as if they would both collapse if one of them moved. Off to the side, the last woman leaned against the wall, by herself, tears openly streaming down her face.

As soon as I entered, all four of them looked up at me, questioning expressions on their faces.

"Are you with the police?" the man asked, his voice dull.

"Better. I'm a private investigator. I've been hired by Gail, Matt's mom, to find out who did this to him. Would you all be willing to talk to me?"

"Anything to help someone get to the

bottom of this," the man said, standing. He held out a hand, which I shook. His hands were calloused and rough, but his handshake was not overly firm. Friendly. When he stood, he was obviously far taller than he had looked folded over in the office chair. He stood probably six foot four, and his skin had the deep tan and slight leathering of someone who spent nearly every day outside. Brown eyes looked out at me from behind long lashes, and his shapely jaw meant he was quite handsome. He wore a pair of black shorts and a navy button-down shirt embroidered with the company logo over his heart. "Reggie Fowler."

"Charlie Gibson. Were you on the boat with Matt today?"

Reggie shook his head. "No. I captained one of the other boats today. Here at Zodiac, we have two catamarans. Every day, each one goes out on a different cruise. One heads to Lanai; that's the one Matt captained today. I took another group up to Honolua Bay."

"The rest of us were on the boat with Matt today," one of the two women huddled together said. She was also tall, standing nearly six feet, and all legs. She had on a pair of cargo shorts and an open white shirt over a one-piece black bathing suit. "Everything was normal. I don't understand how it happened."

"Can you walk me through the day?" I asked gently.

The other woman nodded. She was around my height, dressed the same as the other woman. "Katrina's right. Everything was normal. We showed up here at six thirty and started getting the boat ready. The weather was perfect. Matt came in here and looked at the maps. He said the weather was fantastic. We could go out to the shipwreck on the far side of Lanai."

"Was that your normal route?" I asked.

"No," Katrina replied, shaking her head. "The water is almost never good enough to go there. I've worked for this company for three years now, and I can count on one hand how many days the winds have been good enough for us to go over there without any problems."

"It was perfect," Reggie agreed. "I've rarely seen weather this good."

"So you took a different route from normal," I said.

"That's right," Katrina said. "Normally we would go to Manele Bay, or Club Lanai."

"And everything was fine en route?" I asked.

"Yes," the other woman said. "Nothing out of the ordinary at all. Everyone was in a great mood. After all, how could we not be? The water was perfect. We were going to see somewhere cool. Selina had never even been there before."

"It's true," Selina confirmed.

"We arrived at the spot right on schedule. And of course, when we got there, we all wanted to go in. Matt dropped the anchor maybe a hundred and fifty feet from the shipwreck, in the sand. Andi, Selina, and I helped the guests get ready, and then we all went into the water," Katrina explained.

"Everyone went in?" I asked.

"I think so." Selina frowned. "I don't think anyone stayed on the boat. It's not mandatory to go in, of course. But almost everyone does, at least for a few minutes. Katrina, Andi, and I go in too. It's a nice perk of the job. And that way, not only can we lead anyone who wants a bit of a guided tour, but we can keep an eye on everyone to make sure no one gets in any trouble. Matt stays on the boat and starts on lunch. The salads and desserts are all prepared on land ahead of time, but the coconut chicken is cooked on board during the snorkeling. Then, when we get back on board, the three of us serve everyone lunch while Matt pilots the boat back to Maui."

I looked over at Andi, who was obviously the woman sitting on the floor, silently sobbing, her head buried between her knees. My heart went out to her.

"We stayed out for an hour and fifteen minutes, which is standard when we're only doing one stop," Selina explained. "I was the first one who came back to the boat, after about an hour. I wanted to be available to help anyone who needed a hand getting back on board. I climbed out of the water then went to find Matt. And that was when…"

Selina trailed off, and she covered her mouth with her hand as tears welled up in her eyes.

"I know it's hard, but I need you to tell me everything you can," I said gently.

"He'd been stabbed. He was lying on the deck, a knife sticking out of him."

"Did you recognize the knife?" I asked.

Selina frowned slightly with uncertainty. "I don't know. I didn't really look at it that closely, to be honest. I just saw the blood. And that he was dead. His eyes. I'm never going to forget what they looked like. My first aid training kicked in. I went to see if he had a pulse, but he didn't. I used the radio to call for help. Then I waved Katrina and Andi over. I told Andi to take the passengers to the beach. I didn't want her to see him. I didn't know what else to do."

"I didn't even know he was dead," Andi said from her spot on the floor, so quietly I could barely hear her. "Why didn't you tell me?"

"I wanted to protect you," Selina said, her voice cracking. "I'm sorry."

Andi rose to her feet, her eyes flashing with

anger, before she stormed out and burst into the outdoors through a fire door at the back of the room.

I followed her. Andi obviously had something to say.

Chapter 6

"Hey," I called after her as she left. "Andi!"

The woman turned and glared at me. In her early twenties, with black hair cut in a trendy, shoulder-length shag, she was short and slim, with dark, hooded eyes that betrayed both anger and sadness. "What do you want?" she snapped. "Is it not enough that Matt's dead? Why even bother? What's the point? He's not here anymore."

Her anger dissolved into sobbing, and I walked over to her and instinctively took her in a hug. Instead of pushing away from me, Andi collapsed into my arms, her tears soaking through to my shoulder. "I can't believe he's gone," she wailed into my arms.

"I know. I'm sorry," I cooed softly, stroking her back as I held her close. I knew what it was like to lose someone you were close to, and I let her free the emotions she obviously needed to get rid of.

After a few minutes, Andi pulled away, wiping tears from her eyes. "Sorry," she muttered. "I'm not... I don't..."

"Don't worry about it," I interrupted, taking her gently by the elbow and leading her to a nearby bench. We now faced the large parking lot that served the businesses in the area. Andi collapsed onto the old, white-painted wood, making it creak slightly. I joined her and waited while she collected herself.

After a minute or so, she took a deep breath. "They didn't care about him, you know?"

"Katrina and Selina?"

"And Reggie. They're pretending, now, of course. But he was just a coworker. They didn't really know him. Not like I did. He was the sweetest person. How is it that I'm talking about him in past tense? Matt loved the water. He loved being on the boat. This was his dream job. The fact that he was out here when someone killed him. I just can't believe it."

I chose my words carefully. "You're probably best suited to help me figure out who did this, Andi. Can you answer my questions?"

"Yes. You're obviously smarter than those idiot cops who came to speak to us. They talked to us like one of us murdered him. I think they were ready to haul me off to the station when they found out I was his girlfriend, only I have five witnesses who saw me in the water when he was stabbed. There was a family from France who specifically wanted to see a reef shark, so I guided them away from the boat and toward a nearby cluster of corals, figuring they had a better chance."

"You weren't on the boat at all, then."

"No," Andi replied, staring down at her hands, which she wrung in her lap. "I wish I had been. Maybe I could have stopped…"

She trailed off, and I gave her a moment to collect her thoughts before I continued. "Whoever killed Matt had to be on the boat with you that day," I said softly.

The plan to visit the new site had been made that morning. No one could have organized to be at that site ahead of time. Whoever killed Matt had to have been on that boat. I wasn't sure how Andi would react to that statement, but she just nodded.

"I know. I thought about that too. That's what makes this so hard, you know? Whoever it was, I saw them. I probably spoke to them. Someone that I interacted with killed the person I was closest to in this world. How do I come to grips with the fact that I spoke to the person who killed Matt and didn't even know it at the time?"

"You couldn't have known. I've interviewed quite a few killers now, Andi. Believe me, you can't know. Most murderers don't walk around with a sign around their neck reading 'I've killed someone.' This isn't your fault."

Andi inhaled sharply. "Yeah. I've been telling myself that. But I should have known. What kind of girlfriend does that make me?"

"A normal one. One who doesn't see ghosts around every corner. Now, you understand the implications of the killer having been someone on the boat. It means you knew everyone there. Can you help me figure out who would have wanted to kill Matt?"

Andi nodded. "I will. But I'm not sure how much use I'll be. Who could have done it? I have no idea."

"From what you said when you came out here, it sounds like you don't think much of his coworkers. Why not?"

She waved a hand. "Oh, they wouldn't have *killed* him. Nothing like that. It's just that Reggie was pretending he and Matt were best friends when the police came by. They weren't, though. They were coworkers. Nothing more. Two people who went to work together and captained different boats. It just felt like Reggie was trying to capitalize on Matt by pretending they were best friends. It made me so mad."

"Yeah, that happens a lot when someone dies. People want to center themselves."

"It's not fair. Matt legitimately had friends. Good ones. Like Konane. I don't know if anyone has even told him what happened yet."

"Okay. But Reggie was on a different boat. There's no way he could have killed Matt, right?"

"Yes. He couldn't have done it."

"What about Selina and Katrina? Do you know of any issues Matt had with them?"

"No. None. I like them both. They're nice, you know? They've been friends forever, from what I've heard. Katrina's the one who brought Selina in when they needed a new guide. Whoever's on board with them is kind of the third wheel, but who cares? It's a job. They both do it well. Things are fine."

"And Matt never told you about any problems he had with them? They've never said anything, or you never saw anything between them that looked off?"

"No. They're both good at the job. Matt had to correct Selina on a few things when she started, but it was nothing out of the ordinary. Teaching her how to tie the boat to the dock properly, that kind of thing. Just normal new job stuff. She was apologetic for not knowing how to do it."

"Okay. What about the passengers on the boat? Did Matt know any of them, by chance?"

"That's the thing," Andi said, sounding confused. "I don't think he did. So why would any of them have killed him? Could it have just been some psycho? But then how would he get away?"

I had been asking myself the same question.

"Were there any other boats in the water when you were there?"

"No. It was just us. The shipwreck is pretty far out on Lanai. Isolated, even for people on the island. Have you been there before?"

"Never. I've heard about it, but that's it."

"The boat was a World War II fuel tanker made of concrete and steel. After the war, they deliberately ran it aground off the shore of Lanai, near what's now called Shipwreck Beach. Because so much of it was made of concrete, the steel parts have rusted away, but it's still there, just off the reef. Over the decades, coral has built up on and around the hull, and it's become a part of the environment. It's a few hundred feet from shore."

"Would someone have been able to swim from shore to the boat and back?"

"Sure. It would have been difficult but not impossible. After the alarm was raised, we guided the guests to the beach, where we organized for a bus to come pick them up and bring them over to the ferry to get back to Maui. That's how we got back. It's not a difficult swim if you've got flippers."

I paused while I collected my thoughts. That meant the killer likely swam back to shore but still must have been on the boat when it left Maui.

"Was there anyone on the beach when the boat arrived?"

"No. Not that I saw, and I had a good look around. It was only my second time ever coming to this spot. The winds and currents normally don't allow it. We generally sail to the other side of the island."

I nodded. That confirmed, then, that whoever killed Matt was on the boat when it left Maui. "Do you have access to a manifest with the names of everyone who was on the boat?"

"Of course. For a snorkeling crew, making sure we've got everyone on board is paramount. We do head counts before and after every stop and do a double manifest check before leaving the harbor. I can get you that list. But Matt didn't know anyone. They're all tourists. How would he?"

"He was born and raised on the island?"

"Yes, raised by his mom."

"I met Gail earlier."

"Then you know how wonderful she is. His dad walked out when he was a baby. Couldn't handle parenthood. But Gail did such a wonderful job of making sure Matt never felt like he lost out. He grew up in Kihei, in the same apartment where Gail still lives, and he loved the water. One of their neighbors convinced him to go into boating, and he was hired here about seven years ago. He loves it. On the water is where Matt was destined to be."

"He didn't have any family, or connections to people on the mainland?"

"No. His grandparents died a few years back. Gail has a sister, but she doesn't have children. That's all the family."

"And I assume Matt isn't in touch with his father's side?"

Andi shook her head. "No. He moved to Oahu after abandoning the family, but I think that's the last they ever heard from him. Matt certainly never mentioned anything else about him. Matt was all about Gail. He wanted to make her life great, you know? Pay her back for raising her so well. He wanted to buy her a better apartment. A new car. He wanted her to have the world, since she gave up so much to give it to him. His father didn't factor into his life at all. Even if Matt knew where he lived, he wouldn't go see him. And he certainly would never have looked for him."

"What about other problems in Matt's life? Was he having issues with anyone? Even if it doesn't seem important, I need to ask you. I can never know what's going to lead me to his killer."

Andi bit her lip. "There was one person, actually. I don't know if they had issues. But Matt was spending a lot of time with him recently, on some sort of business deal. The last few times I saw them talking, they looked serious. You know, like things weren't going very well."

"Okay. Who is it?"

"Anthony Bradley. Tony."

"Do you know what his business deal was?"

Andi shook her head. "No. Matt didn't want to talk about it. He said it was still early days but that it was a big opportunity."

"Do you know where I can find Tony?"

"His day job is as a real estate agent out in Kihei. He's the agent working on leasing the office space upstairs; that's how he and Matt met."

I jotted down Andi's words. "Okay, thanks. Was there anything else going on in Matt's life? Anything out of the ordinary at all, even if it didn't seem suspicious?"

"No," Andi said, turning to stare at me with question marks in her eyes. "There was nothing. I swear. I can look through his things."

"Did you live together?"

"Yes. We have a little ohana in North Kihei."

In my experience, an ohana was a strictly Hawaiian thing—a small house, usually a studio or one-bedroom, built behind someone's home. Basically, an aboveground, detached version of a basement suite. They were fairly popular on Maui, and while I couldn't exactly say they were affordable anymore—what was?—they were certainly one of the cheaper options for living on the island.

"Any issues with the landlords?"

"No, they're great. A young family; they have two kids and a couple of cats. We share the yard, and we have cookouts together pretty regularly. If they need a babysitter on short notice and either one of us is available, we're always happy to step in, and as a result, they give us a small discount on rent. There's no way they'd do anything to Matt."

"All right, thanks, Andi."

She nodded then grabbed my hand, clutching it like it was the only thing chaining her to reality. "You have to find who did this," she implored, her eyes boring into mine for the first time in this conversation. "I know you're going to try, and this is your job, but I mean it. Please, I need you to find out who did this. I need to know who took Matt away from me. I know you're going to look at me and think I'm just young. We weren't even engaged. But we were going to be. We were talking about it. I genuinely, to my core, believed I was going to spend the rest of my life with Matt, and someone ripped that away. Ripped away his future. Can you imagine what that's like? I had made plans with Matt. We were going to go on vacation in a few months. We were going to get married. He wanted to start his own company, so he could eventually buy his mom an apartment.

And someone just took that all away. Now all I have are memories. Everything he was ever going to be is in the past."

Tears streamed down Andi's face. The heartbreak resounded in her voice. This was a woman who was hurting. "I promise you," I told her, meeting her gaze. "I will do everything I can to find who did this. I've done it before, and I stop at nothing. I promise."

"Thank you," she whispered. "A part of me wonders if I'm being greedy. Should I ask you to put yourself in harm's way for the idea of closure? For the idea that whoever did this will also suffer for having done it? It won't bring Matt back. Maybe it makes me a bad person."

"No. Wanting justice doesn't make you a bad person. Justice is the natural order of the universe. Wanting chaos would make you bad. Wanting revenge? Questionable. But wanting someone to pay for the crimes they committed? You're not a bad person for that."

"I wonder if justice is enough, though," Andi said, staring down at the ground beneath her feet.

"It won't feel like it right now. Believe me, I know how you feel. You want to tear the world apart to bring Matt back. I get it. I really do. But that will pass. I know it's a cliché to hear that time heals all wounds. And it will never truly fix things. You're going to love Matt until the day you die. I know you will. But this pain? This feeling that you want to Hulk out and destroy everything and anyone that did this to him? That will eventually fade away. And when it does, you'll be able to focus on the good things. You'll be able to celebrate his life, instead of wanting to avenge his death."

"I hope you're right," she whispered.

"Can I take you somewhere? Home? To family?"

Andi shook her head. "No. The police wanted me to stay here. They wanted all of us to stay here, while they took our statements at the front. I can't leave yet."

"Okay. Why don't we go back inside? Is that okay with you?"

"Yeah," she said in a small voice. "At least they're all leaving me alone. I snapped at them. That wasn't fair to them, was it?"

"They'll understand, given the circumstances. And if they don't, then they don't matter."

Andi stood and looked at me, offering me the smallest of smiles, obviously all she could manage right now. "Thank you. For everything. For looking for Matt but also for this conversation. I really needed to get some of this off my chest."

"Of course."

"Do you think the police will help?"

"They'll do what they can." I did mean that,

but honestly, I wasn't holding out much hope. This was going to be a tough case.

"What's your email address? I can get you the manifest of everyone who was on the ship today."

I gave Andi my card, and she slipped it into her pocket. I led her back to the rear entrance of the store and knocked on the door, which Reggie opened a few seconds later.

"Sorry, Reggie," Andi muttered as she walked past.

"Don't worry about it," he replied. "I asked the cops to speak to you next, so you can go home."

Andy nodded and trudged back to the wall she'd been sitting against before. She wrapped her arms around herself, like she was trying to keep warm, even though it had to be nearly a hundred degrees in here.

I knew from experience it would be a long time before she felt warm again.

Chapter 7

About a minute later, the woman that I'd seen interviewed at the front of the store returned, and the police motioned for Andi to follow them. She joined Katrina and Selina and looked at me curiously. "Are you looking into Matt's death?"

"Yes," I said. "I'm a private investigator working on his mother's behalf. Were you on the catamaran today too?"

"No," the woman replied. "I run the office. I'm Isla. Isla Beasley."

"Charlie Gibson. I have to ask—I've met all of you, but who owns the company?"

"A man named Jerry Evans," Reggie replied. "He's normally here, but he's away on business right now. Looking at buying a new boat in California. He left yesterday morning and will be back tomorrow."

"Okay, so you manage fine without him here?"

Isla smirked. "We're used to it. Jerry is far from the most hands-on boss. But I like it, personally. Better than being micromanaged."

"I saw the 'check in here' sign above your desk. Does that mean you met everyone who went on the boat today?" I asked Isla.

"Yes. They arrive here and check in with me. I mark their attendance, and when everyone is ready, the captain and crew for each trip comes out and greets everyone."

"How many passengers were on Matt's boat today?"

"Eighteen. Each of our two catamarans can hold twenty-four people, including the crew. And we limit ourselves to six passengers for every guide, to ensure the safety of our guests and a personalized experience."

Eighteen people. Plus four crew. That made twenty-one people who could have potentially killed Matt.

"When they checked in, did you notice anybody acting suspiciously? Or even just out of the ordinary? Did anyone ask questions about the crew? About Matt specifically?"

Isla shook her head slowly. "No. No, I can't remember anything like that. They were all normal. Just tourists, you know? One of them wanted to know the specifications of the boat, but he was just a run-of-the-mill boat nerd. Told me all about the sailboat he had back in Maine. One woman seemed nervous. She asked about the crew, but she only wanted to know about their first aid certifications. Were they technically lifeguards? If she had problems in the water, would anyone notice?"

"I know her," Katrina said. "She spoke to me when we were on the boat. She was very nervous, but I think I put her at ease. I took her with me when we first went out, along with the rest of her family. Even held her hand for a while. After about five minutes, she seemed to be a lot more comfortable, and she told me she was good to go from there. She wasn't a bad swimmer at all. She'd just never been snorkeling before and had never been in the ocean. She'd only ever swum in indoor pools."

"What happened after Matt was found?" I asked, looking at Katrina and Selina.

The two women glanced at one another, and Selina answered. "I radioed for help straightaway. I called Katrina over, and told her to get Andi to help her take everyone to shore. The police arrived after about ten minutes and had a bus brought over. Everyone boarded the bus, and we were taken to town, where we checked in at the police station. Then, we were taken to Manele Harbor, and from there, the ferry took everyone back to Maui. We came back here."

"Did you check to make sure everyone who'd boarded the boat was on the bus?" I asked.

Selina nodded profusely. "Oh, yes. Trust me, making sure everyone is where they should be is the single most important part of this job. I did a check before we left the beach, before we left the police station, and before we boarded the ferry. Everyone was there. I would stake my life on it."

"Okay, thanks. Just one more thing: Reggie, why are you here and the rest of the crew that was with you aren't?"

"The snorkeling tour that stays on the island leaves later. It means we return later, but because of the interruption caused by Matt's death, we didn't know what had happened when we got back. The others left, but I still had some work to do on the boat. So, I was still here when the bus with all of Matt's boat's passengers came back. That's when I found out, and I figured I should stick around in case the police wanted to talk to me too."

"Right. Here's my card. If any of you think of anything else that could help me figure out who did this, could you let me know?"

I passed my business cards around then

headed back out the same way I'd exited with Andi. Then I walked back around the building to get to Rosie's SUV. This case was interesting. Matt had been killed on the boat. There were no boats nearby. No one was on the beach. Whoever killed Matt must have been on that boat when it left Maalea Harbor.

That left the staff and the tourists. It was risky, whoever had done it. They were an enclosed group. A limited number of people could have committed the act. Not to mention, the aftermath had required a lot of guts as well. After killing Matt, someone who had just taken another human being's life had to jump back into the water and pretend to be a tourist, or guiding tourists, and go about their life like nothing had happened.

If they'd swum to shore and gotten back to Maui on their own, their absence would have been noticed, and they would have immediately flown to the top of everybody's suspect list. That meant they had to have killed Matt and then re-joined the group like nothing had happened.

If that wasn't psychopathic behavior, I didn't know what was.

I immediately put the car into drive and headed to the hospital. I knew Jake needed time to rest, but hours had passed, and I wanted to see how he was doing. On the way, I took a little detour, heading in the direction of the airport to stop by my favorite spot in Kahului—the little lot across from Costco that was home to Manuela Malasada and Kraken Coffee. Both were located in little trailers. I grabbed a white chocolate macadamia nut iced mocha from Kraken, one of their signature drinks and, in my opinion, the greatest coffee on the island. Then, I went to Manuela and got a dozen filled malasadas to take to the hospital.

The Portuguese-style donuts were made fresh and filled with cream. During the plantation era, workers from Madeira and the Azores came to Hawaii and brought their traditional desserts with them. Malasadas specifically quickly became a Hawaiian favorite, and the sweet, crispy, delicious doughnuts could now be found all over the islands.

While traditional malasadas were not supposed to be filled, here in Hawaii, sweet creams were a common addition, and I picked an assortment of chocolate haupia—otherwise known as coconut, lilikoi, mango, cookie butter, guava, and ube cheesecake for the half dozen I bought. Manuela made the best malasadas on Maui, in my opinion. Or maybe it was Sugar Beach Bake Shop. Or T. Komoda. Okay, there were a lot of places on this island that did great malasadas, and I knew Jake would appreciate some after a few days of hospital food.

I pulled up to the hospital a few minutes later and checked all my mirrors before getting out. I hated feeling like this. Like I was constantly being watched. Being in danger, knowing that someone out there was trying to kill me.

The memory of having been Tasered and kidnapped in this very parking lot came flooding back, and I hardened my jaw. I wasn't going to let these assholes ruin my life. Or end it. I was going to find them, with Dot and Rosie's help, and I would make sure they spent the rest of their lives in jail. At the very least.

After stepping out of the SUV, I entered the hospital and went down the hallway to Jake's room. I stepped inside, and my heart thumped as I gazed at him. He was lying in bed on his side, facing me, looking at something on his phone.

As soon as his gaze landed on me, he smiled and set his phone on the table next to him.

"Just who I wanted to see."

"Me, or the malasadas?"

"*Porque no los dos?*" Jake replied, quoting a line from an Old El Paso commercial that had been ubiquitous during our childhoods.

"I figured since you've got a hole in your butt, you should get a dessert that also has a hole in its butt," I announced, opening the box and handing it to Jake.

Jake flashed me a mischievous grin. "There's a

joke to be made about chocolate filling, but I'm way too classy to make it. Unlike my girlfriend, who brought me donuts with a hole in the butt to match mine."

"I guess technically there's two holes in your butt right now," I pointed out.

Jake plucked a mango malasada from the box and took a careful bite. "I can't believe I'm the sophisticated one in this relationship," he said through the sweet pastry. Then, he licked the filling out suggestively, maintaining eye contact with me the whole time.

"You're so gross."

"You started it."

"Okay, I guess I did," I conceded. I placed the box on the side table next to his bed and then grabbed the cookie butter donut for myself.

When I chomped down and began to chew, Jake asked, "Did Dot and Rosie find anything?"

"Yes. Sort of. Dot hacked into the rental car company's database and found the fake ID one of them used and the credit card associated with that identity. Unfortunately, it hasn't popped up anywhere else yet. She's got a flag on it, so if they use it, she'll be notified. But so far, they're in the wind."

"Damn it," Jake muttered, looking over at his IV. "I need to get out of here."

"No, you need to rest, so that your second butt

hole doesn't start leaking something much more gross than the inside of a donut."

"These donuts were a terrible idea."

"They were a very funny idea."

"That have led to some extremely gross jokes."

"I'm only hearing positives here. Seriously, though, how long have the doctors said you need to wait before you can be discharged?"

"They want to hold me for observation for a few more hours. Luckily, the bullet never hit anything vital, so it was pretty simple. They would have released me already by now if I hadn't left, but they're worried about internal bleeding caused by my running around. They're also a little worried about infection, and Zoe gave me a very stern lecture about making sure I come back if I start to feel any sort of chills."

"That does sound like her."

"I don't mind. You're alive, and that's what matters. I'd have gone through a dozen surgeries if it meant saving you."

"I'm glad you're still saying that after the donut jokes."

Jake rolled his eyes at me. "You're ridiculous."

"I also have another case."

His mouth dropped open. "You do not."

"I do."

"Do you not think you should be focused on the gangsters trying to kill you?"

"I am focused on them. But short of driving around this whole island all day, on the off chance that I see them, I don't have anything to do right now. Dot is the one who's handling all the surveillance."

"Yeah, about that—where did she learn to hack a car rental company's database?"

"I have no idea, and I'm afraid to ask."

"Fair enough."

"So my other option is to hunker down in my apartment and wait for them to find me, while I let all the thoughts in my head build up. Do you know how bad of an idea it is for me to be left alone with my own thoughts?"

"Immediately yes," he said. "You should offer up your brain to psychology while you're still alive."

"They'll probably name a disorder after me. That would be pretty cool."

"The fact that this is something you want to achieve is probably a sign that you're right."

"A Charlie complex. That has a nice ring to it."

Jake laughed. "I think everyone who's met you knows you have a Charlie complex. For example, we're now getting off the point, which is that you should not be taking a case right now."

"I have to. For one thing, as you said, Charlie

complex. I'm not going to hunker down in the apartment and wait for them to find me. And I also don't want to wander around the island, trying to find a needle in a haystack. I need to do something productive. Besides, this murder is interesting."

Jake's eyebrows rose, and he shifted slightly, wincing at the movement. "Murder?"

"On a boat, off the coast of Lanai, with no one except the crew and a group of snorkeling tourists nearby. So it had to be someone on the boat who killed him."

"That's an interesting situation," Jake muttered.

"Right? And everyone on the boat was accounted for. They all went to the police station and left their information. But one of them is a murderer."

"You do realize the station on Lanai has their own detectives who can look into this, right?" Jake asked.

"I do. But Gail, the murdered man's mom, is a friend of Dot's. They go back a long time. And besides, this is going to be good for me. I need to do something while I'm waiting for the gangsters to come out of hiding."

He sighed. "I know. I get it. But as your boyfriend, I have to admit, I really just want to roll you up in a ten-foot-thick layer of bubble wrap and lock you up somewhere well out of harm's way until they're found."

"And that's sweet, but I would literally go insane if you tried. I'm going to do this. You just have to accept it. Besides, it won't be that dangerous, compared to some of the other cases I've worked. Whoever killed Matt had to be on the boat when it left the harbor. That leaves a very limited suspect pool."

"True, but from what you've told me, one of them was way too calm, cool, and collected after they killed a person. You're dealing with a psychopath."

"I agree. And I honestly think they might be less dangerous to me right now than some of the other people on the island."

Jake sighed. "I guess we both know that nothing I say is going to stop you from doing this, so I might as well regain my strength."

"Pretty much. Anyway, right now I was going to hang out with you until you get freed from the hospital. I'm waiting for Matt's girlfriend to send me the manifest with the list of everybody who was on that boat. I figure I can't do anything else until I get it. And my hands are sore."

"Let me look?" Jake asked, and I held them out to him. The bandages covering them were starting to leak, but worse than that was the feeling that I was still wearing gloves that were about three sizes too small. If I tried to extend my fingers all the way, the skin pushed back against me, tightening.

"I'm going to call the nurse in so she can rewrap this for you," he said.

"No, it's okay," I protested, but Jake had already mashed the call button.

A few minutes later, a friendly redhead in her forties arrived, and she took one look at my hands before declaring that she couldn't allow me to leave here before she redid the dressing for me.

When she finished, I was just opening and closing my hand in a fist a few times when Liam, Jake's partner, raced into the room.

And when I said raced, I meant waddled in as fast as he could, for a man who looked like an M&M in human form. And not the sexy one that weirdos on the internet got hot and bothered over.

That said, while Liam was normally the kind of cop who didn't seem to let anything faze him— including crime—he was obviously upset right now. His small, beady eyes were locked on Jake, and Liam's mouth, usually flecked with icing sugar from a recently consumed donut, was pressed into a hard line.

"Word's just come in from the captain. A body's just been found at an abandoned construction site outside of Kihei, and it's looking potentially suspicious."

Jake shook his head. "We can't take it. They're about to release me, but there's no way I'm cleared for field duty. Besides, I want a bit of a break right now, with what's going on with Charlie."

"Believe me, Jake. We want this one. The vic had an eye gouged out."

Chapter 8

I GASPED SLIGHTLY. "DO YOU HAVE A PICTURE?"

Liam looked over at me, the hard line of his mouth curving downward into a frown. He had never liked me, but that was fine. I didn't like him either.

"No. But given what Jake's told me about what happened to you…"

Liam trailed off, and I looked down at my hands. A million thoughts spun through my head. There was no way I would go down for murder. That was basically the biggest positive to come from this. I had a textbook case of self-defense if the guy had died from the wound in his eye.

"What was the cause of death?" Jake asked, as if he could read my thoughts.

"Cops on the scene aren't sure," Liam replied.

"It might be blunt force trauma, might be infection. I guess the ME is going to have to make that call."

"Tell the captain we're taking it," Jake said, groaning slightly as he shifted his weight and rose to his feet. "We can be there in an hour."

"Are you sure?" I asked, immediately reaching out an arm to help stabilize Jake as he got up from the hospital bed, wincing.

"Yes. This is obviously one of the men who took you. Liam and I need to be on this case."

Jake looked at his partner, who nodded curtly. "I'll let the captain know."

He turned and left the room, and I grabbed Jake's clothes from the side table. There was a hole in the back of his pants, surrounded by blood. "It's got to be him, doesn't it?"

"Two people with gouged-out eyes turning up on this island within a day of each other? Yeah, it's him," Jake said, his voice hard. "I need to be on this."

"I know you're going to refuse, but I'm coming with you."

Jake opened his mouth as if to argue. Then he looked at me, his eyes boring into mine for a few seconds. "Okay, fine," he finally said.

My eyebrows flew skyward. "Really?"

"I know you well enough to understand I'm not going to be able to stop you. And frankly, this group is dangerous. They need to be stopped. I'll get raked over the coals over this at the trial, if it comes to that, but I'm not worried about that right now. I'm worried about keeping you alive. Your friends seem to be able to help. Your being there might help us find them faster."

"For what it's worth, I've been telling you this for months."

"Just take the *W*, will you, Charlie?"

"Okay. But just so you know, you can't wear these pants out."

Ten minutes later, we were speeding down the highway. Rosie kept a change of clothes in the back of her car in case of emergency, so Jake was now wearing a pair of pastel purple sweatpants that belonged to a woman in her seventies who stood half a foot shorter than him, which meant the hem only reached about six inches above his ankles. The look was not very fetching, but it was better than his other options of "blood-soaked-and-bullet-hole-adorned slacks" and "hospital robe."

He and Liam had left in the police car, and they were stopping off at Jake's place so he didn't have to show up at the crime scene wearing Rosie's pants. I followed them in her SUV. Just under an hour after we left the hospital, we pulled up to the crime scene.

A chain-link fence blocked off the construction

site along Ohukai Road, on the eastern side of the highway. Red dirt spilled from the side of the road onto the asphalt, and the hills of upcountry rose in the distance. Yellow police tape across the construction site's now-open gate flapped in the wind. A half dozen vehicles were parked along the side of the road. On the chain-link fence was a sign that might have been green at one point, with white lettering. It read Gaffey Contracting. Maybe. Coffey Contracting? Something like that. Next to it was a faded old plastic sign zip-tied to the fence warning intruders to keep out.

Someone hadn't listened.

I stepped out of the SUV and watched as Jake gingerly got out of his side of the car. He leaned against the frame and winced. I pretended not to notice. He was doing this because of me.

"What have we got?" Liam asked, taking control as the three of us were led past the police tape onto the scene.

I took it all in. This site had obviously been abandoned quite some time ago. A foundation had been put in for what looked like some sort of commercial building, judging from the size and the location. A bit of rebar stuck up from the concrete slabs building the walls, but that was it.

Off to the side lay a small pile of scraps of wood that had obviously long since been abandoned. Mounds of dirt abounded. There was no trailer, no machinery. No sign that anyone had been here in months. Maybe years.

A man I didn't recognize walked up to Liam. The uniformed officer was in his twenties and carried himself with his shoulders back, all business. This was a man who wanted to be promoted.

"Detectives," he said. His eyes caught mine, but he didn't dare to ask what I was doing here.

"Officer Cooper. What have we got?" Jake asked.

"Body was found behind the foundation, about three hours ago. A few local *keiki* thought they'd come over here to play hide and seek. They found the body, got scared, ran home, and waited for the first one's mother to get home from work, which took her about an hour. They told her what they found, and she immediately called us. It's over here."

The man turned and led us behind the foundation. Even with the injury to his glute, Jake was still able to keep up with Liam's normal pace, and we soon found ourselves looking directly at the man I knew only as Sean.

"Still haven't identified him," the officer said, but his voice sounded far away. I was entirely focused on the body in front of me.

His face was convulsed into an expression of

horror. He had died in pain. Or terror. I hoped it was both. The gang had made no effort to cover up his body; he was splayed out on the ground with one arm above his head, like he'd been dragged with it.

The other thing that immediately stuck out was that his hands were missing.

"Have you found those?" I asked, motioning to his wrists.

"No," the officer said.

"I want you to get a team together and search this whole area," Liam ordered. "All the way to the highway."

The officer nodded curtly and headed off to do as Liam had ordered.

"They won't find them," Jake said quietly.

"You don't know that. They might get lucky."

"Not these guys. They're an experienced gang from out of state. They took the hands so that fingerprints would be out of the question. My guess is they're in a bag weighed down with rocks at the bottom of the ocean."

I nodded. "I agree. And there's a bit of blood on the ground where his hands were but not that much. It's almost just oozing out. I think they were cut off here, but he was already dead."

"I don't see any obvious gunshot wounds. He might have died of an infection. This doesn't look like he's had it taken care of," Jake said, grunting as he crouched down over Sean's face. "They must have realized if they showed up at the one hospital on the island, they'd be caught, and that there was no way he was in any shape to fly elsewhere."

"So they just waited for him to die?" I asked. "That seems quick. I thought infections took a lot longer to set in."

"Since you took out his whole eye with a broken beer bottle, I'm guessing there were a lot of access points for bacteria to get in," Jake said.

"And if we're lucky, the cause of death will be blunt force trauma or something," Liam muttered. "Make it a bit easier for everyone if these gangsters just killed each other."

Jake had obviously updated Liam on everything.

"We need to look for identifying marks," I said. "Anything that could lead us to where they were staying. They're going to have been careful. We won't get lucky enough to find a hotel room key, but you never know."

Jake frowned. "We can look, but it's unlikely. There are tire marks, but we already know what rental car they've got. And I wouldn't be surprised if they swap it out for another one today, just in case. After all, they know I must have seen the plate number."

My eyes widened. "You're right."

Jake tilted his head to the side. "You better not be thinking what I think you are."

"I totally am. Don't worry. I'm just going to follow them if I find them. I don't want to take them all on myself. Not yet."

"Don't do it, Charlie," Jake warned.

"Try to stop me, donut butt," I replied with a grin as I turned and began racing back to the SUV.

"I'm vetoing that as a nickname, *immediately*," Jake called after me.

My heart pounding with excitement, I hopped into the car, threw it into drive, and sped back toward the highway, dialing Dot and putting her on speaker as I did.

"What have you got?" she answered.

"Sean's dead. Looks like maybe an infection to the eye. They cut off his hands to make identification harder, but it's definitely him. No question about it. They dumped his body at a construction site a few hours ago."

"Are you in danger of being arrested?" Rosie asked. Obviously, I was on speaker.

"I don't think so. Liam and Jake are the detectives assigned, and even Liam seems to get it. And you know he'd throw me in jail immediately if he could. Jake obviously caught him up."

"That's good," Dot said.

"Besides, they don't know for sure how he died yet. Honestly, it wouldn't surprise me if they realized he was knocking on the gates to hell and decided to speed things up a bit."

"It couldn't have been much more than twelve hours between when he attacked you and his eventual death. That's quite quick to die from an infection but not unheard of," Rosie muttered, almost to herself. "I suppose we'll see. But the important thing is that you're not caught in the middle of this. And to keep you safe."

"Jake said something that made me realize they're probably going to swap rental cars," I said.

"I know. I have the company's database flagged. But we don't know what ID they're going to use."

"We don't. But I'm driving up there now. If I can physically see them check out and give you a license plate number, then we can track them that way."

"If you're willing to do that stakeout," Rosie said. "Are you sure you can keep your cover?"

"Yes. I'm in your car, remember? They're not going to see me. I'll be subtle. And I won't follow them too closely. I just want to get the license plate."

"Okay," Dot said. "As soon as you have it, let me know. I can track them from there."

"Got it."

"And Charlie?" Rosie asked.

"Yes?"

"No matter what happens, you need to know that man dying wasn't your fault. Even if he died from an infection. It was self-defense."

"Thanks," I said. As much as I knew, deep down, that this wasn't my fault at all, I also knew the human brain was a mess—especially mine—and it was good to get a reminder before I fell down the rabbit hole of wondering if I was actually responsible for Sean's death, even if he did deserve it.

"I also went down and spoke with Matt's coworkers. Whoever killed him had to be on the boat. There's literally no way anyone else could have done it, short of taking a jet pack in, or falling onto the deck from the sky. And people in the water probably would have noticed the former. I'm waiting for an email from his girlfriend with the list of everyone who was there. I expect it'll come in soon. When I get it, I'll forward it to you."

"Good. I'll run all the names on it and see if anyone sticks out."

"It's weird, though. All the passengers were tourists. There were only three other crew members, and one of them was his girlfriend. I know it's not impossible for one of them to have done it, but if you were going to murder someone in a remote location where he had to know his killer, wouldn't you wait until there was more than a one-in-three chance of you being the primary suspect? Especially when one of those three is the person most statistically likely to have done it?"

"Not everybody premeditates their murders," Rosie pointed out. "It could be that Matt got into an on-the-spot argument."

"I think that's unlikely, but not impossible," I said slowly. "The other three guides were all supposed to be in the water. It would have been strange for one of them to be back on the boat. They could have been asked for help or guidance by customers. Besides, the crew weren't supposed to be out near Lanai that day. It was only because the weather was good. If you're going to plan a murder, you want to do it where you know the territory. Where you realize what's going to happen. I think if it was one of the staff, they would have picked a different day if it was premeditated."

"Which means either it *was* a spur-of-the-moment thing by a crew member who returned on board for a yet-unknown reason, or a premeditated murder by one of the passengers hiding a connection to Matt," Dot said.

"Exactly what I was thinking. So we either have a passenger who's pretending to be someone else and had a secret reason to murder Matt, or a crew member who wasn't getting along with him. I need to find out which one it was."

"Did you find any motive?" Rosie asked.

"Nothing solid, but there are a few leads I can follow. His father abandoned the family when Matt was young."

"I remember him," Dot muttered. "A scoundrel from the start, that man. I wasn't the least bit surprised when he ran out on Gail. I told her not to have a child with him, but she wouldn't listen to me. He was a philanderer, the kind of man who thought being married meant he could continue living like a bachelor but with someone to clean up after him."

"Ugh," I said with a grimace.

"Joe was the same, and he's one of the many reasons why I've been very happily single since the day I left. Anyway, I knew Vincent going out every night for drinks with his buddies meant Gail wasn't happy. Then she got pregnant. She was thrilled. Vincent wanted kids in the same way all deadbeats want children: they want to shove their sperm in something and claim their line is continuing while putting absolutely no effort into actually raising the child. Gail thought when Matt was born, it might get Vincent to grow up a little. But it didn't."

"And so he left," I finished.

"After about a year, maybe two, if I remember

right. They had a big fight that night. The police were called. Vincent said that if he was so unwelcome to see his own son, none of them would ever see him again. And he stuck to his word; I certainly haven't seen him since."

"It would be weird for him to come out of the blue like that and murder his own son, whom he hadn't seen in over two decades," I pointed out. "But, if he'd used a fake name, there's no way Matt would have recognized him. He wasn't in touch with his father at all, according to the girlfriend, and had no interest in changing that. Besides, what reason would the father have to come murder his son? There's no motive at all. He hasn't been in his life in twenty years; he's had plenty of time to move on."

"Perhaps, but it's best not to eliminate him completely," Rosie said.

"I agree. Still, I think it's unlikely. I still have to talk to his best friend, and he knew a real estate agent that he was involved in a deal with. Neither one of them was on the boat, but they might be able to help with a motive, once we've got that list of people who were on board."

"Great, keep us informed," Dot said. "And Charlie?"

"Yeah?"

"Be careful."

"I will."

"And if you damage my car, you're paying for it," Rosie warned.

"Don't worry. I have absolutely no intention of ending up in a chase today," I replied with a smile. I ended the call and turned my attention back to the highway. I had some gangsters to find.

Chapter 9

I PULLED INTO A PARKING SPACE AT KAHULUI
Airport right near the exit of the underground
parking lot, which meant anybody exiting would
have to drive right past me. Of course, if these
guys were going to one of the lesser-known
companies, a little bit farther away from the termi-
nal, I wouldn't see them. But the first time they'd
gone with one of the majors, so I figured they'd
probably do the same again, especially since it
would involve a shorter walk.

Pulling into my parking spot, I kept an eye on
the lot in front of me while I checked my email.
Andi had forwarded me the list of the names of
the people who had been on the ship with Matt, so
I immediately sent that off to Dot then glanced at
the list myself.

I didn't immediately recognize any of the

names. It made sense; they were all tourists to the island. Or at least, they were supposed to be. I began doing a quick Google search, stopping occasionally as cars drove up toward where I was seated, making sure no one in the any of the cars was Kyle, or either of the Ham brothers.

But so far, nothing. However, after about an hour, Dot called. I put the phone on speaker as I watched the parking lot.

"What have you got?"

"Seventh name on the list. Calvin Boone. He used to live on Maui, about ten years ago. Got locked up for misdemeanor assault, did a few months."

"Misdemeanor means it wasn't just a consensual bar fight, then. That would be a petty misdemeanor and less than a month in jail."

"That's right. It looks like Calvin had a bit too much to drink at the bar, decided a guy was hitting on the girl he wanted, and decided to express his displeasure with the man by punching him in the face. Other patrons took him down before he could do worse, and it earned him ninety days in jail and a permanent mark on his criminal record."

"He sounds like a peach."

"Great guy all around. As soon as he was let out, he decided Maui was no longer for him, packed it up, and moved to Cincinnati."

"And now he's come back to his old haunting grounds."

"Precisely. He's found himself a new girlfriend, and they're vacationing on the island."

"The question is, then, is Calvin's trip just an innocent vacation where he shows his girlfriend the sights, or did he specifically choose that cruise for a reason?" I asked.

"I'M GOING TO DIG DEEPER INTO HIS LIFE. IF there's a connection between him and Matt, I'm going to find it."

"Thanks, Dot."

"How's the stakeout going?" Rosie asked.

"So far, it's a whole lot of nothing," I admitted. "This could go nowhere. They might have swapped the cars out hours ago. They might not do it at all. Or they could go to a different lot. We'll see, but I'm not giving up just yet. If I can just get a name from them, we can track them down. It's not like I have anything better to do right now."

"I'll continue working down this list," Dot said.

"Got it. Let me know if you find anything."

While Dot did that, I looked up Tony Bradley. That was totally a name that belonged to a guy who played football in high school, whose hairline started making a break for it around age twenty, and who insisted that he was a "nice guy" whom women didn't want before calling them bitches when they rejected him.

It didn't take me long to find an online presence for him. Tony Bradley was a real estate agent who specialized in commercial property. His headshot made him look about thirty, maybe thirty-five years old. His golden tawny skin was flawless, his dark brown hair styled professionally as he flashed the camera a confident smile, facing the camera at an angle with his arms crossed gently in front of him. It was a look that was supposed to say, "I can get the job done, but I'm open and trustworthy," but the crossed arms made him look way too closed off, instead.

His Facebook and Instagram were all professional-only. If he had personal accounts, they were locked down tight; I couldn't find them. But it didn't appear as though Bradley did much business online, anyway. He had very few posts up; the most recent was from two months ago, in which he celebrated the leasing of a property in a small mall in Wailea.

Whatever Tony was doing, he wasn't advertising it online.

The sound of a car's engine began echoing through the underground parking lot, and I put my phone aside and waited for the vehicle to drive past. About fifteen seconds later, it did; I kept my head down, despite expecting it to be yet another family, couple, or single person on holiday, smiling as they exited the airport and got their first real glimpse of this beautiful island.

But no. The face I saw made my breath catch. I hadn't actually seen the Ham brothers in person before. Well, not Connor and Braden, anyway. I had seen their brother Stevie, although he masked his face slightly to try to hide his identity when he robbed the jewelry store I was working at. That was what had started this whole mess; I'd killed him in self-defense.

However, I'd seen their faces in the Seattle papers enough times to know Braden had just driven past me, with Kyle in the passenger seat. And he'd turned and looked right at me as he'd driven past. I froze, like prey caught in a predator's sights. Had he spotted me?

The shining red light and the squealing of the brakes told me that yes. Yes, he had.

Shit.

I immediately mashed the button to turn the car on and threw it into drive. In the parking spot, I was basically trapped. I knew Braden had seen me; there was no point in denying it and leaving myself more vulnerable.

I slammed my foot down on the gas just in time to see the rental in front flash its reverse lights. I peeled out from the spot and yanked the steering wheel to the left, going around the black sedan just as it began reversing. The car launched forward; Rosie had obviously had *something* done under the hood because this thing had more power than any SUV off the lot, short of a Lamborghini.

Did Lamborghini even make SUVs? That was a question for a later time.

I blasted out of the parking garage and merged in with the rest of the cars coming from the airport, my eyes taking a second to adjust to the brightness after having spent a few hours in a dark, cramped underground parking lot. It was now late afternoon, and the sun, beginning to set, shone almost directly in my eyes. I threw on my sunglasses then glanced in the rearview mirror.

The black sedan was about a hundred feet behind me. And I knew if they caught me, I was dead.

I'd been involved in a few car chases in my time, but usually I was the one doing the chasing. I wasn't used to being the prey in this situation. What was the best way for me to get out of this scenario alive? And without scratching Rosie's beloved SUV? Because she was going to kill me if I brought it back scratched up.

Right now, the answer was to keep that gas pedal pressed to the floor. The speedometer crept upward, well above the speed limit. Fifty, sixty,

sixty-five, seventy miles an hour. I weaved around cars like I was in a *Fast and Furious* movie but with more hair than Vin Diesel. And better one-liners.

I flew into downtown Kahului, half hoping for the first time in my life to find a cop ready to pull me over. Or maybe not. Would I be able to explain what was going on in time? Or would I just be putting them in danger too?

I quickly began to consider my options. I could go deeper into Kahului and try to lose them, but that would be tough. Most of the residential neighborhoods in this town were planned—built like long suburban streets without many places to lose a tail.

I could also take the highway down to Kihei, but that didn't seem like a great option either. It would be the world's longest car chase along a flat, expansive highway. And if I hit traffic, I was screwed.

No, my best option here was the Kahekili Highway. Despite the name, it was a narrow, twisty, winding road that linked the north side of the island with the west side, travelling along the edges of cliffs, among some of the island's most rugged terrain, on what was often just a single-lane road full of switchbacks and blind corners, where the slightest mistake meant plummeting to your death on the rocks below.

The road was considered so sketchy that most

rental car companies didn't insure drivers who took it between Kahului and the famous Nakalele Blowhole, but I had a sneaking suspicion that right now, the Ham brothers weren't particularly worried about their insurance coverage.

I drove through Kahului, horns blaring at me as I blew through intersections with minimal warning. I almost crashed into a car turning left onto Waiehu Beach Drive as I spun the wheel to the right, but the driver slammed on his brakes just in time. Glancing through the rearview, I saw the Ham brothers were still behind me.

Before I knew it, I was on the highway headed to West Maui, going through the small area of Waiehu, the closest thing Kahului had to a suburb. Passing by one of my favorite places on the island, Ula'Ula Café, I ignored the 30 mph speed limit signs—I was a strong believer in the idea that if you didn't see them, you weren't technically breaking the law, an idea that Jake had very passionate thoughts about—and pressed on. I leaned forward, gripping the steering wheel tightly. There was less traffic up here, but the roads were narrower, the shoulder barely more than a few inches of grass. There was no room for error.

An engine rumbled as we kept going, and I watched as the headlights of the sedan grew larger and larger in my rearview. They were obviously sick of this and trying to end it. I sped up even faster, just as the front bumper of the sedan nudged the back of Rosie's SUV. Luckily, momentum was on my side, and I sped away just as we reached the Waihe'e Point lookout, which marked the beginning of the twisty, winding parts of the highway where, I hoped, I could get away. This was my home. I'd grown up here, and I knew these roads better than anyone else. Advantage, Charlie. If I could lose them on this highway and get down into Kahului on the other side, I could turn off the highway and escape for good.

I took the first few corners as fast as I could. On the side of the road, a white wooden fence with missing slats that had been completely knocked down in parts was the only barrier between the rocks below the road and me. There was no way that fence could stop me if I went through it.

I forced myself to look away from it as I continued, and three corners later, I checked my rearview. They were still on my tail. Damn it. As it turned out, they were better drivers than I thought.

I pressed the gas pedal and took another breath as we continued. It was slow at first, but I began to lose them. They were thirty feet behind me. Then fifty. Then sixty. Then, as I turned the next corner, I could just see them coming out from the previous one.

Then, nothing. I was getting away. I grinned as my plan worked. As we crossed over the ridge, the terrain began to change. The dirt up here was red, iron-rich. It was what Mars would have looked like if someone dropped a tropical forest onto it. This stretch had a couple of turn-offs that I could have tried, but they were too exposed. I didn't have enough of a lead on the other car; they would see me when they went past.

I reached the sleepy village of Kahakuloa and sped through, causing a couple of tourists trying to jaywalk with their arms full of Ululani's shave ice to jump out of the way. One of them sent their shave ice flying, and it fell right through the sunroof and landed in the back seat with a splatter.

Oh, I was not going to have a good time when I had to explain this to Rosie.

I waved an apology to the couple as I flew past them, and then I continued. I was almost home free when suddenly, a loud bang came from the hood of the car, and the engine began to slow down.

"No, no, no," I screamed, slamming my fist on the dashboard as if that would fix anything. I had maybe—*maybe*—a thirty-second lead on these guys. This couldn't be happening.

But it was. The car slowed. I mashed the start button but got nothing. Whatever it was, it was broken. Pulling the car over to the side of the road, I had a decision to make.

I was near the trailhead known as the Acid War Zone Trail. I abandoned the car on the roadside and immediately began to run down the trail.

Chapter 10

THE ACID WAR ZONE TRAIL WAS SO-NAMED because closer to the water, which was home to the famous Nakalele Blowhole, the landscape transformed into a water-battered landscape reminiscent of something out of a sci-fi video game.

However, the first part of the trail was a dirt road along the grass; I'd be spotted almost immediately, but there was no getting away from that now. I raced along the dirt trail frequented by dirt bikes and ATVs. The sun was just setting, creeping behind the ocean against the far horizon and transforming the sky into a gorgeous pink-and-orange hue, but I was more focused on the path ahead of me. After about a minute, I dared to look back and spotted two heads in the distance running toward me.

They were coming. I swore and hurried along the trail. I wasn't a runner. I wasn't even a jogger. I was more of a gentle walker. But adrenaline was a hell of a drug, and Sha'Carri Richardson would have had trouble catching me as I raced along the path. Before long, the path forked, and I headed northeast into the trees. Only a few seconds passed before I broke out of them and reached the old lighthouse, which marked the northernmost point of West Maui. It wasn't much to look at; the lighthouse was only a few feet tall, just a giant metal post with a couple diamond-shaped bits of other metal attached to it.

As soon as I emerged from the trees, the wind began whipping at my hair and body. The sun had well and truly dipped over the horizon by now, and the pinks and oranges turned to deep blues and purples, the light fading fast. The sky would be pitch black before I knew it.

Being out here at night would be even creepier for the two Seattleites. As I passed by the lighthouse without giving it a second glance, the landscape transformed into the acid-war part of the trail. The rocks along here had been weathered down by the water, which beat along the shore and was taken by the wind, creating some of the cool patterns in the rocks far from the edge of the water.

The black and gray mass looked like coral, in a lot of ways, or like, well, acid had been dropped on them. The closer I got to the water, the louder the roar of the waves got. The rocks here differed in size, providing plenty of space to hide, crouch down, and keep my pursuers from finding me.

If I had to, I could hide here all night until they got confused then try to race back up to the road and get help. There was no cell phone coverage down here, but if I got back to the road, I could probably get a bar or two.

I raced along the rocks, using the taller ones for cover. I'd come this way a hundred times in my life; Nakalele Blowhole was a popular tourist site, and anytime Dad's family came over to visit from the mainland, we always made a trip out of coming here. It usually meant Zoe and me—Zoe was always invited, since I had no cousins to hang out with—running between the boulders, with my mother calling after us to be careful.

We were. We stayed on the trails, but we raced along them like they were nothing, and even though over fifteen years had passed since I'd done it, Mother Nature generally changed pretty slowly, and it all came flooding back to me like it had just happened yesterday.

I scratched my leg on an errant rock jutting out slightly, swore to myself, and kept going. It was getting dark very quickly. After a while, I threw myself behind a large boulder just off the trail and paused. The wind whistled loudly between the rocks, and the waves pounded against the shore just a few feet away. I tilted my head to the side, hoping to hear the scramble of feet, or better yet, shouts of pain, coming from behind me. There was no sound. Were they still coming after me, or had they given up?

I had to assume it was the former, so I continued, heading toward the blowhole.

Nakalele Blowhole was located just a few feet from the edge of the water. The blowhole was also one of the most dangerous parts of this trail. Even though the idea that maybe you shouldn't get too close to the giant hole that shot out hundreds of gallons of water every few minutes shouldn't have been the most difficult thing to understand, a few Darwin Award winners always decided to test their mettle against Mother Nature and inevitably lost.

The hole wasn't cordoned off or anything. It was just a gaping hole in the middle of the rocks. Walled in on one side by a cliff that stood about twenty feet high, the cliff offered a great vantage point for people who just wanted to sit nearby and get the occasional mist of water. Adventurous kids, teenagers, and some adults went closer, most stopping about ten feet away from the hole, getting soaked when it eventually roared to life.

Now, however, it was nighttime. All the tourists were long gone. It was just me—and two men who were actively trying to kill me. I figured the blow-hole was my best shot. I knew it was there. I was counting on the idea that these guys hadn't bought a guidebook before they hopped on that plane.

I scrambled along the rocks, heading to the blowhole. Carefully avoiding the gaping hole in the ground, I ducked behind a nearby boulder and waited, my heart doing its best to escape the confines of my chest.

About five minutes passed before I spotted them; they were on the cliff above the blowhole. I could just make out their silhouettes against the moonlit sky. One of them had his phone out and was using its flashlight feature. As soon as I saw them, I rose slightly, just enough to let them make out my figure.

One of them nudged the other, and he pointed toward me. If they said anything, I couldn't hear them. Did they have a gun? I wondered. They might not have, since they were just going to swap their rental cars. Still, it was probably safest to assume they were armed.

The two men scrambled down the edge of the rocks and headed toward me, and as soon as they did, I stepped out from my hiding spot. The moon offered a little bit of illumination but not much. I had to use this to my advantage.

"You," one of them shouted, struggling to be heard over the wind. He was about twenty feet from the blowhole. I figured it was Kyle, but his voice was getting caught in the wind, and I wasn't one hundred percent sure.

"You killed my brother," the other one shouted.

Okay, yeah, the first one was Kyle.

"He shouldn't have tried to kill me first," I shouted back.

"You killed Sean," Kyle shouted at me.

"Ditto. You can always turn around and go back, you know. You don't have to try to kill me." The ground began to rumble slightly beneath my feet. I took a couple of steps back, and the men moved closer to me. "You can go. Or you can die. Those are your two options."

Kyle laughed and pointed something at me. For a second, I thought it was a gun, but a flash of yellow gave it away. It was that fucking Taser.

Why did it always have to be a Taser?

Before I had a chance to duck away, pain coursed through me once more. I fought to stay conscious, trying to ignore the pain. The outside of my vision began to darken, but I gritted my teeth, choosing by sheer will to stay awake.

"What the fuck? Why is she still up?" I just heard Kyle ask.

"I'm going to finish her off myself," Braden said, stepping toward me.

The two men stepped forward, there was another rumble beneath me, and this time, Mother Nature attacked.

Or, since we were on Maui, the credit belonged to Pele's sister Namakaokaha'i, the Hawaiian sea goddess who was responsible for the ocean swells and the tides.

Just as the two men reached the blowhole, it exploded.

Braden had been just near the edge, and he caught the bulk of the blast. Water shot fifteen, twenty feet into the air with a roar, taking him along with it. He let out a scream as the water sent him upward, soaring high.

Kyle had been a step behind him. Not close enough for the blast to send him skyward but close enough that it caused him to stumble. He lost his footing on the slippery rocks, and as the water from the blast receded, he fell to the ground.

The water had worn down the rocks right near the hole to the point that walking on them was like walking on ice. With a scream, Kyle slipped and fell into the hole, swallowed into it and disappearing without a trace.

I knew full well he would never be seen again.

"Welcome to Maui, bitch," I muttered under my breath.

I looked around for Braden, whom I'd lost track of when the sudden blast of water sent him flying. My eyes scanned the area and, a few seconds later, landed on him. He was about twenty feet away, spread across a rock near the edge of the ocean.

As I got closer, I realized he was screaming. Clutching his leg, he writhed on the ground in pain, only inches away from the ocean that beat away at him.

His eyes turned and landed on mine a few seconds later. "You bitch," he snarled. "You fucking bitch. You're going to die. I'm going to fucking kill you."

He reached toward the back of his pants. Maybe he had a gun after all. I wasn't sure, but I also wasn't about to wait to find out.

"You first," I replied as I kicked his shoulder, hard.

He let out a scream as he rolled over the edge of the rock and into the water. It wasn't a big drop, only probably a little less than ten feet. But it was the middle of the night, the black water was angry, and Braden only had one good leg.

If he was strong enough, he could get out. But I wasn't going to let him kill me.

"You bitch," I heard him shout once more on

the wind as I turned and headed back away from the shore without another glance. The sound of Braden Ham's struggle against the ocean was lost to the noise of nature, always so much more powerful than mankind, no matter how much we pretended otherwise.

Chapter 11

I scrambled along the main trail to get back to the road above. After about five minutes, the adrenaline of the day's events began to wear off, and reality started setting in on my body. I was shivering. Sure, it was Hawaii, and even at night, it didn't get especially cold here. But I was soaked through to the bone, and the wind whipped against me, making the air feel so much colder than it actually was.

Pain seared through the cuts I didn't realize I had on my legs. I must have scratched myself a few more times than I'd noticed at the time. My muscles were sore, thanks to the Taser.

I focused on just getting back up the hill to the road. One step at a time. One rock at a time. This time, I used my phone's light to help guide me in the dark; I wasn't worried about being followed anymore. A few times I'd checked behind me, just to make sure, but there was no sign of Braden. If he managed to climb out of the ocean, he'd be found in the morning, and I could make sure he was arrested.

But I didn't think that was going to happen.

Eventually, I scrambled up to the road. I continued walking down along the highway, hoping to flag any passing cars, but this part of Maui was practically deserted at night. After a few minutes, I reached Rosie's abandoned car and climbed inside. I pressed the start button, hoping the car would magically come to life so I could turn on the heat, but no luck. The engine was dead.

I sighed and slumped against the seat then began to look around. Despite her former life as a Soviet spy, she was now the most responsible person I knew. And that meant, while she wouldn't have anything cool in here like a grenade in the glove compartment, there would probably be a first aid kit somewhere.

I got out and went to the back. A few minutes later, I returned with everything I could dream of. Jake still had the pants of her extra tracksuit in here, but I was wearing the jacket now. A first aid kit gave me antibiotic cream and bandages for my scratched-up legs, and she even had an extra blanket, along with a full 24-pack of unopened water bottles and a six-pack of granola bars.

I settled into the driver's seat with the granola bars and began munching one while I composed a text. Service dropped in and out, but staying put and waiting for the single bar that could send my message to Dot would have to do.

At Nakalele. Braden Ham and Kyle are dead, and so is Rosie's car. It wasn't my fault, I promise. Come get me?

I got the red exclamation point of failure twice upon sending the text, but the third time, the whooshing sound of the message going out into the world reached my ears, and I breathed a sigh of relief, leaning back against the headrest and closing my eyes for a few seconds. Dot and Rosie would get the message, and they would come and get me.

I downed three granola bars before my friends got there. Why did Rosie have to be so reasonable? You know what would have been a better choice? Fruit Gushers. Or Dunkaroos. Did those even exist anymore? I made a mental note to check Safeway the next time I was out grocery shopping. But the high-protein oat-and-raisin granola bars did nothing for me.

I should have taken the rest of those donuts off Jake. I bet Liam ate them.

My food thoughts were interrupted about forty minutes later by a familiar-looking set of headlights turning the corner. That could only be Queenie.

I stepped out of the car and waved as Rosie pulled the car over to the side of the road and stopped.

Dot jumped out of the passenger seat and came toward me, Queenie's headlights emphasizing the lines of concern etched all over her face. "Are you all right?"

I nodded. "Yes. But Rosie, you need to buy better treats for your car."

"They're not treats. They're emergency supplies." Rosie shot me a pointed look telling me that I should know better.

"Emergency supplies don't have to taste like sawdust. Ever heard of Goldfish? Or peanut M&Ms?"

"These bars are designed to maximize energy in a situation where you can't simply text your friends to come and rescue you," she said. "Now, stop talking about food. What happened?"

"In the car. I'm freezing, and I want to go home. Also, we're going to have to call to get this one towed. It broke all of a sudden."

"What happened?" Rosie asked, looking over at it.

I shrugged. "I was just driving, there was a clunk, and the engine cut out."

Rosie pressed her lips together. "The dealership and I will be having words tomorrow, then."

I got into the car, wrapping Rosie's emergency blanket around my legs like a makeshift skirt to keep my legs warm. "I lured them out to the blowhole. They're both dead. At least, I think they're dead. We'll know tomorrow if we hear about an emergency rescue up here."

As Dot drove home, I recounted the whole story in detail. The roads were quieter than normal at this time of night, the highway nearly deserted. I began to shiver as the whole reality of the situation began to set in. Braden and Kyle were dead. So was Sean. That meant three of the four gang members we knew had come over here to try to kill me were now dead themselves. Only Connor Ham was left. And he probably wouldn't be thrilled that I'd killed a second brother of his.

Even if technically, I'd given him a chance.

"I got their license plate number," I said. Their abandoned car had been left only a few feet from where I'd parked. "We can track them that way. Although now, it's only Connor."

"Still. If a card was used in the name of whoever rented the car, we'll find them," Dot said, pursing her lips. "You're very lucky."

"I know," I said quietly. "I didn't think they would see me. And as soon as they did, I had to act."

"You have good instincts," Rosie said approvingly. "Staying in that stall would have likely meant your death. They would have trapped you almost immediately."

"Do you need us to take you to the hospital?" Dot asked.

I shook my head. "I don't think so, thanks. I've seen enough of that place for a lifetime. I think I just want to go home."

"We're staying with you tonight," Rosie declared. "After all, Connor is going to get suspicious soon. We don't know what the other two told him. They could have called from the car. He might be going after you."

I nodded, running my hands up and down my face. I knew Rosie was right. All I wanted was to go home, collapse into my bed, and sleep for fifteen hours. And then maybe take a shower to wipe all of the grime of the day off me. I was so grateful they were willing to come stay with me so I could do that without having to worry about my safety.

"I need to text Jake."

I pulled out my phone and composed a text. I paused, my fingers hovering over the keys. How was I supposed to convey that I was fine and also let him know what had happened without typing it all out? I eventually decided simplicity was best.

Hey. Are you home? I need to talk to you. Everything's okay. I'll be back in about half an hour.

His reply came through a couple of minutes later. *Still at the station. Hoping to get away in an hour or so. I'll come by when I'm done. You sure you're all good?*

I'm not the one with a hole in my butt.

Technically, neither am I. That's what the surgery was for.

Did they leave the bullet inside of you? I can't believe I haven't asked that yet.

I've never seen a surer sign that you love me. For the record, they did.

You're going to set off the metal detectors at the airport for the rest of your life.

I always knew my ass was explosive.

There's a Taco Bell joke to be made there.

Oh my God. I'm going back to this new murder case. It's less gross than you are. By the way, you're off the hook. The ME says they eventually decided to put Sean out of his misery. He was suffocated; he didn't die from the infection.

At least that was one less problem to worry about.

"Jake says Sean was killed by the others," I told my friends.

"That's a relief, at the very least," Rosie said. "In this situation, you're trying to estrange your-self from these men. Having been involved in the death, even in a situation where it was obviously self-defense, wouldn't have been ideal."

I nodded. At least there wouldn't be anything to worry about when it came to the other two either. No one else had been near the blowhole. Their deaths would be chalked up to accidents, if their bodies even washed up at all.

They'd never be connected to me.

Dot drove Queenie to my apartment complex and dropped Rosie and me off. "I'm going back to my computer. Now that we have the license plate they used, I'm going to see if I can track down the one Ham brother who's left. You'll be fine here with Rosie, Charlie."

"Great. Call us if you find anything. Or just come over."

Dot nodded then peeled out of the parking lot. She was enjoying getting to drive Queenie.

Rosie scanned the scene like an experienced secret agent before ushering me toward the door. "It's late. We should get inside."

"Okay, James Bond," I muttered under my breath.

"I heard that."

Of course she did.

We went inside, where I found Zoe sitting on the couch, cuddling with Coco with a cup of tea in front of her.

"Hi, Zoe," I said to her when we came in.

She immediately looked me up and down. "What on earth did you do?"

"I don't look that bad, do I?"

"You're wearing a tracksuit top I've never seen before, you have on a blanket for a skirt, your hair looks like you're doing some Albert Einstein cosplay, and I'm pretty sure I spotted a bandage on your leg from beneath your skirt blanket when you took that last step. I've known you for almost our whole lives, Charlie. This is a bit much, even for you."

"Fine," I admitted, taking a deep breath while Zoe stood. Rosie immediately headed to the kitchen and got herself a glass of water. "I ended up getting chased halfway across the island by one of the Ham brothers and the other guy who kidnapped me. I had to go down the Acid War Zone Trail to get away from them, and then they both got blown away by the blowhole."

Zoe gaped at me. "They're dead?"

"I think so."

"Are you okay? I mean mentally too."

"Yeah. Believe me, it's a lot easier to justify what I'm doing when I remember how close I was to them killing me less than twenty-four hours ago. And I know they would have if given the chance. Even after he was about to go into the water, Braden Ham still told me he was going to kill me. He reached behind his back. I think he had a gun."

"That's terrifying. Come on, show me the bandage."

Zoe motioned for me to sit at the dining table, and I did as she ordered, groaning as I sat down on the chair. The more time passed, the more my body came back to reality, and that meant all the pain the adrenaline had been hiding was coming to the forefront. Layering on top of the pain from the other day. I was basically a pain lasagna at this point.

"At least you covered up these scratches," Zoe said as she looked at my leg, carefully peeling off the gauze. "Did you put antibiotic cream on it?"

"I did."

"This could be cleaned better. Hold on."

"By the way, you're going to have to restock your first aid kit," I said to Rosie.

"As I would have expected. That's why it's there. In case of emergencies."

"Oh, and also, don't be mad, but there might be some melted shave ice in the back seat of the car." I fluttered my eyelashes and gave Rosie the sweetest smile I could.

In response, she raised her eyebrows slightly. "Melted shave ice? Do I even want to know how that happened?"

"The alternative is digging bits of a couple of tourists out of the grill, so trust me, this is going to be better."

"I knew I shouldn't have let you borrow my vehicle."

"In my defense, I hadn't planned on ending up in a car chase with them. I was just supposed to be doing a stakeout."

"I'm not sure that's the best defense I've ever heard," Rosie replied. "Frankly, I'm more disappointed that the car failed on you. I had it serviced last week."

"We should get it towed before Kyle and Braden are declared missing," I pointed out, grabbing my phone. "Let me text Olivia."

"That's a very good idea. I should have left my car with her after I went to the dealership. They threaten your warranty if you don't get it done at an authorized location. Of course, I suppose the insurance is more important than the warranty when you let Charlie borrow your car," Rosie added with a smile.

I stuck my tongue out at her and pulled out my phone. Olivia was a friend of mine and a wizard with cars. She lived in a rural neighborhood outside of Kahului, along with her giant Rottweiler, Egg McMuffin—who went by Egg—and a small collection of cars she was always working on.

I sent a text, hoping she would get it soon, since cell service wasn't exactly the most consistent on her part of the island.

Hey. So, Rosie's car broke down near Nakalele, and we need to get it towed to your place so you can have a look. Is that okay? ASAP would be best.

To my surprise, Olivia responded almost immediately. *Sure. I have a truck. I'll go get it now. Tell Rosie to come by in the morning if she can, and I'll have a look at it.*

You're the greatest.

Always happy to deal in flattery.

"The car is taken care of. Olivia's getting it now."

"Good. The less this can be linked to us, the better," Rosie said.

Suddenly, someone knocked on the door.

The three of us froze. I'd never been gladder that Coco was a worse guard dog than the Pokémon Snorlax. Rosie immediately motioned for Zoe and me to head to the hallway. I scooped up my dog while Rosie carefully snuck to the door, taking it at an angle. On her way, she noiselessly slid a chef's knife from the block in the kitchen, holding the weapon behind her back as she checked the peephole.

I hoped the last Ham brother, Connor, wasn't hunting us down.

Chapter 12

LUCKILY, A SECOND LATER, ROSIE RELAXED AND
opened the door to allow Jake to enter. My shoulders released tension I didn't realize they had, and
I raced forward and wrapped myself in his arms.

"What happened to you?" he asked as we
pulled apart. He looked me up and down.

"I guess no one is ready to accept that I'm in
my crazy cat lady era and this is just what I look
like now?" I asked. "By the way, are there any
donuts left?"

"No, we ate them all."

"You say 'we,' but I bet it was Liam. I'm
starving."

"You had three granola bars in the car," Rosie
pointed out.

"The calories don't count if the food doesn't
taste good," I shot at her.

"I assure you, that is absolutely not how science works," Rosie replied as she returned the knife to its proper position in the block.

"It should be," I grumbled, opening the fridge. I *was* hungry. As it turned out, running for your life was a great way to spur hunger. I emerged with a lilikoi pie—I had a year's worth of free pie and I was going to use it—and a tray of dip, then I grabbed some chips from the cupboard. I poured the chips into a giant glass bowl and slid everything to the middle of the kitchen island for everyone to share.

"What happened, Charlie?" Jake asked, grabbing a chip and crunching it in half noisily.

I leaned my elbows on the counter and sighed, staring down at the chips while I recounted the whole story once more.

"So they're dead. And Connor is going to come after me sooner rather than later, I think."

Jake's expression was serious. "We always knew he was. This doesn't change anything, besides the fact that there are now fewer of them."

"What happens if those four aren't the whole crew?" Zoe asked. "What if they brought more people with them? What if they realize what's happened, and the rest of the gang comes over from Seattle to avenge them?"

"If we cut off the head, that's it," I said. "The Ham brothers run a tight ship. Everyone knows it.

They're the leaders of that organization, and they're not exactly a sprawling democracy. If you cut off that head, there's no others that are going to sprout up in their place. At least, not here on Maui. I can't speak to the drug business in Seattle. But here? No. Connor dies, and the rest of them will flounder."

"What's happening with Rosie's car?" Jake asked.

"Olivia is taking care of it now. She's going to tow it herself."

"Good. I don't want it there when those men are reported missing, or their car is declared as abandoned. As far as anyone is concerned, you can't be linked to this at all."

"That's what we thought," I agreed.

"We have to assume Connor knows what his brother and Kyle were up to and that he's going to come after you." Jake's forehead creased with concern. "We need to find him before then."

"Dot is on it."

"Good. By the way, don't think I didn't notice the knife you had behind your back when I came in," Jake said, turning to Rosie.

"I'm just an old woman, trying to protect Charlie."

"Right. Because of the three of you, the one who's easily into her seventies is the one who should be most likely to defend against an intruder. Don't worry, I won't ask too many questions. I'm just glad you're here for Charlie."

"I'm staying the night, just in case. And if you ever say that I'm easily in my seventies ever again, you're the one who's going to need protection."

Jake lifted his hands in front of him in apology. "I'm sorry, I meant thirties."

"Much better."

"At any rate, your plan is smart. I think we will have a bit of time up our sleeves but not much. I suspect Connor Ham will start to wonder what happened to his brother. And it's not going to take him long to find you."

"Do you still have the Mace I gave you?" Rosie asked.

I reached into my bag and pulled it out. "Sure do."

"Good. Keep it close to you."

"I think they'll likely have guns," I said. "I think that's what Braden was reaching for in the back of his pants when I kicked him into the water. But I'm not totally sure. After all, why not just shoot me when he had the chance?"

"It was dark, and he was in unknown territory," Jake pointed out, grabbing another chip and popping it into his mouth. "He might not have felt confident in the shot."

"More than that, I believe he wanted to kill Charlie from closer up," Rosie said. "She's caused him quite a few problems. He would have heard from his arrested associate that she set him up with the cocaine in his car. She killed his brother. It was justified, but he wouldn't see it that way. As far as Braden was concerned, Charlie was a problem, and her death had to be personal. They could have just shot her in the parking lot. But they didn't."

Rosie's words made my stomach lurch at the thought of how easy it would have been for the Ham brothers to kill me, but she was right. "And when they did kidnap me," I said, "when it looked like Sean was going to mess me up badly, Kyle started yelling at him. The Ham brothers wanted me to be in good shape so they could torture me before they killed me."

"Oh, Charlie," Zoe said quietly.

At that moment, my phone began buzzing in my pocket. It was Dot, so I answered it and immediately put it on speaker. "You've got me, Rosie, Zoe, and Jake."

"And I've got Connor Ham," Dot replied, her voice betraying her pride at having netted him. "Not physically, of course. But I know where he's staying. The credit card in Kyle's fake name was used to book a hotel room. He's staying at the Maui Diamond."

"Well, I have enough connections there. I could at the very least get him kicked out," I said.

"But I think we should let him be. We can't let him know we're onto him."

"No, I agree. He's in room 342. Thanks to the hotel's security camera footage and their internal security systems, which were stepped up after the bombing, I can tell you he used his key to enter the room six and a half hours ago, and he hasn't left since."

"You're the best, Dot."

"I am, but I never tire of hearing you say it."

"I can have someone stationed outside the resort," Jake said.

"No," Dot immediately interrupted. "Not a good idea. We don't want Connor to think anyone is onto him. He went out of his way to make sure Sean couldn't be identified. He hasn't reported Braden or Kyle missing yet. He wants to stay away from the police, and seeing a presence is likely to spook him."

"If you're not going to involve the police, what are you going to do?" Jake asked, frowning at the phone on the table. "Believe it or not, you can't simply sneak in there and shoot him. I know what he's done, but that's still murder."

"There's a middle ground between letting the police scare him into running away and shooting a man in cold blood, *detective*," Dot scolded. "Obviously, we're not going to just murder him. We don't have a plan yet. But we don't want him to run. Right now, he's on Maui. He's within our grasp. If he leaves the island, then he escapes, and this nightmare doesn't end for Charlie."

At those words, Jake's face rose, and his eyes met mine. He searched my face, and I gazed back at him, silently telling him that I knew what I was doing. As if he understood, Jake gave me a curt nod then turned back to the phone.

"Okay. I trust you," he said. "At least, I trust Charlie. And I feel like surely no one on this island is crazier than her. Even you. Whatever you want to do is fine. For now. What I will say is this: if you get any sign that he's going to leave the island, let me know. I'll make sure he's brought in as a material witness, or a suspect, or something. After all, Sean's death is officially a homicide, and while we can't link it to him yet, I'm working on getting the dental records sent off to Washington and ideally getting a match there."

"He would have left the teeth in, expecting that you wouldn't figure out what state he came from, and that the police wouldn't bother sending the records all over the country just in the hopes of getting an identification," Rosie agreed. "And once you do get that confirmation, you'll have probable cause."

"Exactly. Besides, if we really have no other options, we do already have probable cause. I saw Sean when I went to help Charlie. I would rather not have Connor link the two of us, but if it comes down to it, I can bring him in if that's what it takes to keep him on the island. This has gone on for too long. Charlie deserves to live a life where she's not looking over her shoulder constantly."

"Good. Then we're on the same page for now. And if we need the police, I'll know who to call. But let us handle this for now."

Jake tapped his fingers lightly against the counter. I knew this wasn't easy for him. He was a cop. He was used to taking control, especially in situations that involved the law being broken.

"Trust us," I said. "You have to let us handle this. Let *me* handle this. If we need you, we'll bring you in."

"Okay," Jake finally said, rising to his full stature and rolling his shoulders. He winced slightly and grabbed at his hip, obviously hiding the pain he felt from his surgery. "Okay, I will trust you. But if anything—and I mean *anything*—starts to go awry, you need to call me. I mean it."

"I will," I promised. And I meant it. I knew Jake would go to the ends of the earth to save me if he had to. And I loved him for it.

There was no way Connor would ever leave this state. He was spending the rest of his life in prison, or dead. And frankly, I didn't really care which.

Chapter 13

JAKE HAD TO GO BACK TO THE STATION, SINCE HE was now working a murder, which meant no real time off for at least a couple of days. Zoe was heading off to work, and I got ready for bed. Rosie stationed herself in the corner spot of the couch, where she could glance through the window at the parking lot and still watch the front door.

I was, like, ninety percent sure she had a hidden gun on her somewhere, ready to shoot anyone between the eyes if they came in.

Hopping into the shower and letting the hot water wash away the day, I was sure I wouldn't get a wink of sleep tonight. Not after what had happened. But when I got out and climbed into bed, the exhaustion of the day caught up to me, and my body decided that even though this moment was prime relive-the-awful-moments-of-your-life territory, we were just too tired, and I fell deep into unconsciousness before you could even say "intrusive night thoughts."

When I woke up the following morning, every single inch of my body hurt. My hand felt like it was on fire. My muscles screamed every time I even thought about moving. Pain lasagna indeed.

I half climbed, half fell out of bed, threw on some clothes, and dragged myself out to the living room, where Rose was still at attention, like a statue that hadn't moved in the previous nine hours.

"How did you sleep?" she asked when she saw me, her eyes remaining on the parking lot below.

"I want to say 'like the dead,' but that phrase hits a little bit too close to home these days."

"I'm glad you got some shut-eye. You had a big day yesterday. I'm proud of you, Charlie. But it's not over yet. Dot called earlier. She said she's been scouring the security footage. Connor Ham left the resort last night and hasn't returned."

"He's probably out looking for his brother."

"If he's got a vehicle, she doesn't know where it came from."

"Okay. I'm going to get out of here, so you can get some sleep too. Thanks for staying up all night."

"Don't worry about it." The corners of Rosie's

mouth curled upwards. "If I'm honest, it was a nice reminder of the old days."

"You're the scariest person I know."

"Thank you."

I TOOK QUEENIE, DROPPING ROSIE OFF AT HER place and promising that I wouldn't head home with the Jeep and would call when Olivia had her car ready. In the meantime, I headed to the office listed as Tony Bradley's address.

Tony Bradley worked in a private real estate agency located in the second story of a low-rise office building that looked much like every single other office building on this island. Light-colored exterior, big windows. At the front desk, a tall woman with black hair tied back in a sleek ponytail and a name tag that read Kelani motioned for me to sit down. A minute or so later, Tony came out to greet me directly.

He was taller than he appeared in the photo and friendly, in an overt way that gave off used-car-salesman vibes. His dark hair was slicked back, just as it was in the photo, and he held out a hand with enthusiasm, although I begged away given the bandages covering mine.

He did a double take when he saw them, but recovered quickly, opening his hands and arms out in greeting instead. "Hello, Charlie. It's nice to meet you," he said. "Please, come to my office. I'd love to speak with you."

Tony led me down the hall into a small office that barely fit the desk that composed the bulk of it. However, Tony had obviously made an effort to make the rest of the space more welcoming. The walls were painted a warm eggshell, and on them hung colorful prints from local artists. Lots of hibiscus flowers and palm trees.

"What can I do for you today, Charlie?" Tony asked, a friendly smile plastered on his face.

"I'm here to talk to you about Matthew Hogan."

The smile never once wavered from Tony's face. "Of course. The two of us are business partners. We're working together on a land deal. Are you interested in investing with us?"

"I'm more interested in finding out who stabbed him. Matthew's dead."

This time, the smile collapsed. Tony went from relaxed to anxious, his shoulders tensing as he leaned across the table toward me. "What?"

"You hadn't heard?"

"This is a prank, right?"

"I wish it were." I pulled out a card and slid it across the table. "I'm Charlie Gibson, private investigator. I'm looking into Matt's murder on behalf of his mother, Gail."

Tony picked up my card and played with it, tapping it in his palm as he looked at me carefully. "You're not joking."

"Serious as a heart attack."

"Shiiiiiiit," Tony muttered slowly, under his breath. Then, he looked at me again, his expression hard. "Who did this to him?"

"That's what I'm hoping you can help me figure out. You were in business with Matthew?"

"Yes. Oh, shit. This is bad. This is really bad."

"Investment in property?"

"A land buy up north. It was going to be big. Up past Paia, along the highway. We were gathering investors for it. Right along the beach, we're going to build a luxury resort. Ka'anapali, it's full. But Paia? It's right by the water. I know it tends to swell, but there are still some sheltered coves there. And it's right along the road to Hana. That's one of the top tourist attractions on the island, and you can tell tourists they can get an hour's head start on everyone else. And they're only a ten-minute drive from the airport. Matt saw the opportunity for what it was: a chance for all of us to make a ton of money."

Tony's gaze moved down to the table. He looked sad, and when he continued, his voice was quieter. "Matt wanted to make his mom proud. He wanted to buy her a car. A better apartment.

He wanted to give her the world. We were going to give her that."

I paused for a second and considered Tony's words. "I'm guessing that given your plan, most of the investors involved aren't local?"

"That's right. We're primarily focused on getting investors from the mainland who want a foothold on Maui's red-hot real estate market. We're giving them the opportunity of a lifetime."

"Do you have a list of potential investors?"

For the first time since we started talking, Tony hesitated. Then, he recovered, flashing me an apologetic smile. "You'll forgive me, but our clients, they expect a certain level of anonymity. You understand, of course."

"Of course. I do understand. I also understand that Matt was murdered, likely by someone who came from off this island, and that whoever killed him may have reason to come after you too."

Tony laughed, but the sound was hollow. "Why would anyone possibly want to kill *me*?"

"You tell me. Did you have any problems with investors? Anyone who seemed like they'd be more trouble than they were worth? Anyone who threatened you, or Matt?"

"No, of course not," he replied, just slightly too quickly.

"Here's the thing, Tony: whoever killed Matt did it for a reason. It may not even be one you understand. It may be some crazy idea they've gotten into their own head. But the fact is, someone who's visiting this island killed Matt. Do you really want to take the chance that they're going to be happy killing just one of you?"

"I'll email you the list," he replied, chastened.

"What was Matt's role in this?" I asked. "And yours? Was there anyone else involved who lives on the island?"

Tony was obviously happy to talk about his deal again and move away from the idea that the killer might have been after him. "It was a real team effort. Matt, he had access to all these people via his job. He would meet them on the cruise. The men, especially, they loved learning about how to pilot the boat from Matt. He'd tell them all about the water out here. And the women, they loved how charming he was. And so, at the end of the day, he'd tell them he knew about a great opportunity and send them my way. And I would close the deal."

I shot Tony a skeptical glance. "And Matt's boss didn't care that he was using his business to siphon off investors to your private project?"

Tony shrugged. "Matt said it wasn't a problem. His boss was cool and pretty hands-off. I trusted him. That's what our relationship was based on. Trust."

"Okay. And no one gave you any issues?"

He shifted uncomfortably in his chair. "There was one guy."

"Name, Tony. Give me a name. Whoever did this stabbed Matt in the chest and left him to die on the boat. If he wants you next, he'll succeed if I don't stop him."

"Francis Cooper," Tony finally admitted with a sigh, as if revealing the name of the person who might have killed Matt was a hardship. "But look, you have to understand, the guy was panicking a bit over the project, but it's not like he was a psycho or anything. He was just nervous."

"Okay, what was his problem?"

"He was worried the development wasn't moving fast enough. He was a first-time investor. Lives in—I don't know. Grand Rapids. Something like that. One of those hellhole cities in the Midwest, take your pick. He was the easiest guy to convince to invest in this place. He wanted the money, and he wanted to buy one of the condos. Said he was going to rent it out during the summer and spend his winters here, since his job went remote a couple years ago. Can you blame him? If I spent half a winter in Grand Rapids I'd do anything to get out of there. Anyway, he started panicking."

"Did he have good reason to?"

"No, of course not. Have you ever been involved in real estate development?"

"No," I confessed, shaking my head.

"It's all bullshit. The whole way down. I mean it. There are literally always delays, at every step. There's so much red tape. So many people involved. So many moving parts. There's financing. There's construction. There are numbered shell corporations and more numbered shell corporations. Honestly, when you get a peek behind the curtain, you wonder how anything ever gets built at all. Especially a project of this size. This guy had no idea. I tried to tell him, multiple times, that it was normal. There wasn't anything wrong."

"But he didn't believe you?"

Tony frowned. "Some people are just convinced the universe is out to get them. Francis is on the island now. Came up with his family last week. He stopped by here about a week ago and started yelling at me. He told me he had to hide that he was coming here to see me in person, telling his family they were just going on holiday. I didn't think anything of it. He's just a scared dude. I told him the truth: nothing was wrong, everything was going according to plan, and he was going to have his condo within two years and then a hell of an investment after that. He just had to be patient for a little while longer. Rome wasn't built in a day, you know?"

The corner of my mouth flicked upwards. "Did he believe you?"

"Eventually," Tony said, opening his hands, palms outward. "Or at least, I thought he did. He was a lot calmer when he left this office. I thought it was over. I didn't think we'd hear from him again. Do you really think he could have done this?"

"You've met him. What do you think?"

Tony pursed his lips, considering my question. "I don't know," he finally answered, slowly. "I mean, I'm like anyone else. I don't want to think anyone I know is capable of murder. But Francis was angry. And he's obviously the kind of guy who's used to getting what he wants. He's someone with a temper, and to be honest, those people are the scariest. Because you never know what's going to make them snap, or what they'll do when that finally happens."

"Do you have contact information for Francis?"

"Sure. Yeah. I do. I can get that for you."

Tony pulled out his phone and tapped away at it then scribbled something on a Post-it note, which he peeled off and passed to me.

"Thanks," I said. "What about you? What's your story? Did you grow up on the island?"

"Oahu. Went to Stanford for college, where I

was all-American. Swimming. You know, growing up in this state, you can't avoid it."

"I do my best," I said dryly.

He chuckled. "Me? I love being in the water. Anyway, a rotator cuff injury in training put an end to that career plan, but luckily, I was studying business. Got my degree, came back home, ended up on Maui, and here I am."

"You didn't know Matt before this?"

Tony shook his head. "He was a local boy. I didn't move here until a few years ago. I came to Maui a few times as a kid, but I never met him."

"Just for my own records, where were you yesterday?"

"Working from home," he said with a shrug. "Sorry, I don't have anyone who can back that up."

"Do you know Andi?"

"Matt's girlfriend? Sure, I've met her a couple times. Nice girl. I like her. She's obviously into him."

Okay, I wasn't super worried about Tony's alibi. If he had been on that boat, Andi would have recognized him. But Francis Cooper was a whole other story.

"Thanks," I said, standing up. "If you think of anything else that might help, give me a call, will you?"

"Of course." Tony's voice was tinged with

sincerity as he said, "I really hope you find who did this."

I nodded and left the office, my phone already in my hand. The name sounded familiar. Sure enough, when I scanned the list of people who were on that boat, Francis, Kendra, and Nathan Cooper were three of the names on it.

Chapter 14

As soon as I left the office, I called Dot. "I have a name. Francis Cooper. And family."

"They were on the boat," she confirmed.

"Do you have anything on them?"

"Let me look; I did a search last night into all the families. Where is it? Here we go. Francis Cooper. Wife Kendra. Son Nathan. The three of them are from Grand Rapids, Michigan. He owns a small handful of car dealerships in the area. No criminal records on any of them. How'd his name come up?"

"I just spoke to Tony, Matt's business partner. They're working on a development up on the north shore by Paia. Apparently, Francis was getting a bit nervous about the lack of speed at which things were proceeding. He came and yelled at Tony the previous week, and I'm not sure it was a coincidence that he and his family were on that boat yesterday."

"You're thinking he sent the family out to snorkel while he stabbed the captain? That's cold."

"Tony said he was a bit of a hot-tempered guy."

"Francis certainly sounds like a good suspect."

"Exactly. I'm going to go talk to him now, but Tony only has a phone number for him. Can you get me an address?"

"Sure thing. Give me ten minutes."

About thirty seconds after I ended the call with Dot, my phone buzzed again in my hand. It was Olivia.

Got Rosie's car all fixed up. Feel free to come by anytime.

I glanced at my watch. Only about an hour had passed since I'd dropped Rosie off, and I figured she was probably fast asleep. I knew I would be. I sent her a quick text.

When you wake up, Olivia has your car ready. I can swing by and pick you up to go get it whenever.

I'm ready now, Rosie replied about twenty seconds later. The woman was a robot.

I'll be there in five. I then threw out another quick text to Dot. *No rush on that address. Going to take Rosie up to pick up her car from Olivia's.*

I work better under pressure, but all right.

I smiled at the text and hopped back into

Queenie, making sure to get a good look around the parking lot before I drove off. I wasn't about to let Connor Ham get another jump on me.

I headed over to Rosie's, where she was waiting at the front of the complex, and she sprang into the passenger seat with way too much energy for someone who had been awake for over twenty-four hours straight.

"How's Middie doing?" I asked, referring to Rosie's cat, Threat Level Midnight, a.k.a. Middie. She had belonged to a family who moved out and left her to fend for herself. Then she did, creating quite the controversy in Rosie's complex around thefts that tenants believed other people had committed.

The criminal turned out to be Middie, a cat who had a penchant for open windows and shiny objects. When she was discovered, Rosie decided to adopt the kitten and train her to... Well, I wasn't entirely sure.

Become some sort of assassin cat, I assumed, knowing Rosie.

"It's going well. Anyone who thinks you can't train a cat simply doesn't know how to encourage them. They're perfectly willing and able to please."

"I'll take your word for it. Coco does what she wants, and she's a dog."

"Did you ever try to actually train her?" Rosie asked pointedly.

I shrugged as I turned onto South Kihei Road and headed north out of town. "There was never any real need to. Beyond the basics, I mean. She tells me when she needs to go out to pee, and she more or less comes when I call her. Anything else is gravy. She's not much of a wanderer."

"And that's why my cat is better trained than your dog."

"Showoff."

It took about thirty minutes in the mid-morning traffic to get up to Olivia's home. Deep in the forests outside of Kahului, she lived in a small bungalow that had belonged to her parents, where every spare inch of the driveway was home to a car or seven.

When we arrived, Rosie's SUV looked good as new, gleaming away in the driveway. Olivia came out, dressed in a pair of overall shorts and a graphic tee underneath. Her blond hair was tied back in a ponytail, and a stripe of grease streaked across her forehead as she wiped her hands on a rag.

"If it's not my favourite ladies on the island," she said to us as we climbed out of Queenie.

Egg, Olivia's giant Rottweiler, immediately lumbered over, carrying a slobber-covered ball in her mouth, which she dropped at my feet.

I picked up the ball and hurled it to the other side of the yard, and Egg immediately bounded after it with the kind of awkward enthusiasm only an overly energetic dog could manage.

"How's it going, Olivia?" I asked.

"Can't complain. Except about the person who looked at this car. Did you seriously go to a *dealership*?" Olivia asked Rosie. "I thought you knew better than that."

"I have to, for warranty reasons," Rosie replied. "Believe me, I do know better. What did they do?"

"There was an electrical issue with the ignition and the computer. It's these damned newfangled cars and all the electronics included in them."

"Okay, boomer," I joked.

Olivia laughed. "You're teasing me, but I mean it. Back in the old days, when cars were more mechanical than electrical, something like this couldn't happen. But here, we had a situation where the wires leading from the ignition to the main computer corroded. Given the mechanics, it could have happened anytime."

"It just happened to shut down the engine right when I was in the middle of being chased down by a couple of killers," I said. "Great timing, universe. Thanks for that."

If Olivia was surprised, she didn't show it. "Not exactly an ideal situation."

"So you fixed it?" Rosie asked.

"She's good as new. Shouldn't happen again. Although I will suggest you start bringing your car to me for a regular look too."

"I know. Lesson learned," Rosie admitted. "I didn't think they could do that much damage at the dealership."

"I've seen things happen there that would scare the pants off you."

"Nearly losing Charlie over this car's malfunction has done that. I'll be honest, if she'd died that night because the car I made her take to keep her safe had failed, I never would have forgiven myself. Or that dealership."

My heart lurched at Rosie's words. She didn't usually admit to having emotions. She really did care.

"Luckily, that didn't happen," I said, stepping a bit closer to her. I knew Rosie wasn't much of a hugger. Physical proximity was the closest thing you got when dealing with a former spy.

"I've got a few new fun items I can throw into this bad boy, too, next time you come by," Olivia said, winking at Rosie. "But Charlie's message made it sound like you were on a clock this time around."

"We certainly are. However, when all this is over, I'd love to hear what you've ordered. The extra punch you gave this car is very much appreciated, and I'm sure you've got more up your sleeve."

"That I do."

"Thanks, Olivia," I said, reaching down to throw the ball for Egg again, who had dropped it at my feet and was now standing ten feet away, looking at me expectantly, anticipating the throw, her whole rear end wiggling back and forth with excitement. Her front feet moved up and down as her muscles tensed. They were at the ready, like an athlete's.

I launched the ball toward the back fence, bouncing it off the side of the shed halfway down the yard to confuse Egg, who sprinted after it.

"I appreciate you going to get it in the middle of the night," I said. "That made a big difference."

"No one else ever calls me after ten asking me to go get a car from the middle of nowhere as soon as possible. I always assume the worst whenever I hear from you."

"That's probably a good call."

Olivia smiled, the slightest lines forming around her eyes, betraying that she was a naturally happy person. "Just glad I could help."

"Excellent. Charlie, you take it back with you. I'll take Queenie. You stay safe, you hear?"

"I will," I promised as I tossed Rosie my keys, which she caught one-handed like it was nothing.

"We know where he's staying now. It's only a matter of time."

"It is, but this is also a game of cat and mouse," Rosie replied. "With both players trying to be the cat."

"I'll make sure not to be a mouse. I'll be more like Middie."

"She's much better trained than you are."

I stuck my tongue out at my friend. "I'm taking that as a compliment. Besides, I don't pee in a box."

"Neither does Middie. I've trained her to use the toilet."

"See, that's just weird."

"It saves money on cat litter."

"If I go to your house to use the toilet and there's a cat turd sitting there, I'm just letting you know, I'm leaving."

Rosie shot me a disappointed look. "Do you really think I wouldn't teach her how to flush?"

"Okay, now you've got to be kidding me. There's no way I believe that you've not only toilet trained your cat but also taught her to flush when she's done. There's no way."

"I didn't realize there was a line when it came to training a cat."

I turned to Olivia. "I bet you're on my side on this."

"I mean, do I think a cat being trained to flush the toilet after using it is insane? Yes. Do I also desperately want to see it? Also yes. Sorry, Charlie. I'm on Rosie's side here, just because I want to believe."

"That's what *The X-Files* is for," I muttered.

"I'll send you a video," Rosie said to Olivia.

Her face brightened immediately. "I would love that."

"All right, traitor. I'm going to head off. Thanks again for all of this. We really do appreciate it."

"You got it. Anytime. And stay safe, will you, Charlie? I feel like I only get the smallest glimpse into your life, but every time I do, it feels like you're some kind of super-spy."

"Yup, that's me, for sure," I replied jokingly. Rosie, ever the professional, never so much as blinked.

WE SAID GOODBYE TO OLIVIA, AND I HOPPED INTO the SUV again, pleased to find that she had also gotten rid of the shave ice that had found its way into the back of the car. And the smell. There was no reek of rotting milk and flavoured syrup, dried into the seat and ingrained so deeply nothing short of burning the interior would get rid of it. Instead,

I inhaled deeply to find a faint tace of new car smell.

Olivia was magic.

Checking my messages, I saw Dot had sent me an address: the Cooper family were staying at a hotel in Ka'anapali. She also sent me a photo of the Coopers. Franklin looked to be in his late thirties, with light brown hair just beginning to go gray at the temples. He gelled it high, in a style that was reminiscent of Conan O'Brien but gave the impression he was trying to add a few inches to his height by styling it that way. His smile was way too white, and he totally gave off "car dealership owner" vibes just from the photo.

Kendra, his wife, was about the same age. Her blond hair was cut in a stylish bob that hung just above her shoulders. She had blue eyes and a massive smile, her makeup done perfectly.

There was no picture of the son, but that was fine. I didn't need one anyway. It wasn't as if I thought a little kid was the killer.

I drove over to the other side of the island, deep in thought. Had Francis Cooper killed Matt? Did his wife know about the real estate deal? Was she involved somehow? Did *she* kill him? With luck, I was about to find out.

I parked Queenie in a spot by the beach that I was lucky to find just as someone else was pulling out, and then I entered the hotel. I was on my way up to the room Dot gave me when the Cooper family stepped out of the elevator I was about to enter. I stepped aside, pretended I'd just gotten a phone call, and watched as they headed out toward the beach.

Ka'anapali Beach was the longest beach on Maui. Over a mile long, it had been specifically developed for tourism in the seventies, which was the main reason why this part of the island catered almost exclusively to tourists, with very few locals living here in town. The entire beachfront was lined by resort after resort, and a well-maintained path meandered among them, offering up plenty of options for eating and drinking.

The Cooper family, however, were headed toward the beach. I watched from about thirty feet behind as they walked out to the sand, the little boy, Nathan, running in circles in front of them. He could have been anywhere from five to ten years old—the older I got, the more I realized I had absolutely no idea how to tell children's ages. Either way, he was definitely too young to be the killer. But either of his parents could have been.

Francis twisted the family's umbrella into the sand while Kendra spread out a large blanket and began unpacking items from the bag.

"Nathan! Come here. You need some more sunscreen before you go in the water," she ordered, motioning for her son to come over.

"You can't make me!" the kid shouted, cackling with laughter and racing toward the water.

Kendra sighed and rolled her eyes before beginning to apply sunscreen on her own arms.

"You need to control him better," Francis said, scowling slightly at Kendra.

"I don't see you out here giving me a hand," Kendra snapped at him. "Besides, he forgot his goggles. He'll be back in less than a minute. I guarantee it. Because I know my son."

"Look, can we not do this here? We're on holiday."

"*You're* on holiday," Kendra retorted. "I'm still taking care of two children all day, every day."

Oof. Not everything was going great in the Cooper family marriage. I wondered if maybe this stress had led to one of them taking things out on Matt.

Sure enough, about a minute later, Nathan came running back to the shore. "Mom, did you pack my goggles? I think I see a turtle!"

"I did, Nathan. But if you want them, you need sunscreen."

"I don't want sunscreen. It's gross and icky."

"You know what else is gross and icky? Dying of cancer."

"But Mom, the turtle's going to go away."

"They're very slow. I'm sure you'll find it again."

"Do what your mother says," Francis huffed, and Kendra rolled her eyes behind his back as she squirted sunscreen into her palm and began smearing it on Nathan's back, the boy being resigned to his fate.

"Mom, come see the turtle with me!" Nathan cried out when he was lathered up, rummaging through the bag until he triumphantly pulled out a pair of goggles.

"All right, but remember, we can't get too close. The turtles here need their space."

"I know, I know," Nathan said impatiently, yanking on his mother's arm as she pulled off her cover-up, grabbed her own set of goggles from the bag, and ran toward the ocean with him.

Now was my chance.

Chapter 15

I WALKED DOWN THE BEACH AND FOUND FRANCIS muttering to himself as he looked for something in the bag.

"Francis Cooper?"

The man started and looked up at me, confusion in his face. "Yes?"

"I'm Charlotte Gibson. Private investigator. I'm here investigating the death of Matthew Hogan."

"Who?"

Francis was a good liar. He had waited a split second after I inquired about the name, as if asking himself if it was familiar, and furrowed his brow just enough to look realistic. A car salesman, for sure.

"The guy who got you interested in that real estate deal up on the North Shore. Don't play dumb with me. It only makes you look more suspicious."

Francis's mouth pursed slightly, but he realized he was a man caught. "Why do you need to talk to me?"

"Because someone who was on that boat yesterday murdered Matt, and I think it might have been you."

"Look," Francis hissed, his eyes darting to the water where his wife and son were swimming. "I don't know anything about that, okay? Someone killed him, but it wasn't me."

"Help me believe you. It's a massive coincidence that you would have been on that boat that specific day."

"Yeah, and that's all it is. A coincidence. I won't lie—I booked that company on purpose. And I asked what days Matthew was working. I wanted to be on his tour. But only to talk to him. My family, they don't know anything about this. I figured when they were in the water, I could have a chat with him, work things out."

"You were worried about the speed at which things were moving on this deal."

"Yes. I am. Look, have you spoken to Tony?"

"Yeah."

"Then he told you I'm a novice investor, and I'm just getting cold feet. That I don't know anything. But I'm telling you, that's wrong. He's lying. I might not be a property developer, but I've invested in businesses before. I run my own. I own car dealerships in Grand Rapids. Six of them."

Francis paused, obviously expecting me to fawn over him.

"Cool?" I finally replied.

That seemed to be enough to get him to continue.

"Thank you. I've worked very hard to get where I am. Anyway, I know how this stuff works. And this deal? There's something fishy. I don't care what Tony said. There's too much red tape. There are too many excuses. Nothing's getting done. Whenever I asked for official filings, I got the runaround. You ask me, I think this whole thing is a scam, and I'm out a million and a half dollars. Tony wouldn't admit it to me, and I thought maybe if I could just talk to Matt, he might be a bit more forthcoming."

"Tony told me you left him feeling much more comfortable and at ease with the whole situation."

"Bullshit. Tony knew that was a load of crap. I left because he threatened to call the police, and I didn't want to have to explain this to my wife if she found out about it."

"She doesn't know about the investment at all?"

"It was going to be a surprise."

Now, I wasn't exactly a relationship expert—

although my boyfriend *had* just saved my life after escaping the hospital only hours after being shot in the ass. That had to count for something. But even I knew that hiding a million-and-a-half-dollar investment from your wife under the guise of keeping it a "surprise" didn't have its own chapter in the happy marriage guidebook.

"Okay. Tell me all about this investment. What you learned."

"I found out about it when we were last here on the island. We love Maui, you know? The Caribbean just isn't *American* enough."

I resisted the urge to roll my eyes.

Francis continued, "I want to start working from here every winter. My job, it's become a lot more remote the past few years. I still have to visit on-site from time to time, but I could spend most of the winter here and summers back in Michigan. I said this to Matt, last time we were here. We booked this same company, and I went up to see him. He spoke to me about the currents around here. I have a boat up at our lake house over there, and he immediately recognized me as a man who knew and loved boating."

Oh, man. For a car salesman, this guy absolutely did not recognize when his own strategies were being used on him.

"So he told you about this investment?"

"Yes, although he initially was quite secretive

about it. He mentioned it offhand, and I asked what he was talking about. He told me he shouldn't have said anything, but I pried the information loose from him. A luxury resort on the north shore. I immediately knew I was onto something. I come to Hawaii every year, you know, so it's like I live here. I know the area. This had promise. He had the land. The whole beach would belong to the resort. Guests only. It was perfect, and I immediately knew it would make so much money. I asked if it was possible to invest in it, and he sent me to Tony. Tony gave me all the details. He told me not to rush a decision but to stay in touch, and I did. As soon as we landed in Grand Rapids, I wired over the money."

"And now you think it's a scam."

"I do. I've been swindled. I'm sure of it. And I'm not thrilled. I still haven't told Kendra. You can't tell her. Look, honestly, Matt being dead is a bad thing for me."

"Oh?"

"He was worth much more to me alive. As long as he and Tony were around, I knew one of them had my money. Even if I had to take them to court, I could get some of it back. Maybe even all of it. But dead? No. Matt's useless to me dead. I wouldn't have killed him, even if I wanted to."

"Anger can cloud good judgement," I pointed out.

"I know. But I'm telling you, I didn't do this."

"So tell me about what happened yesterday on the boat."

"We went to a special place. That sunken ship off the coast of Lanai. The crew were all really excited; they'd only been there once or twice before, ever. The currents make it hard to navigate there in normal conditions, you see. It's got to do with how the winds circulate around the islands."

Great. Now this guy was mansplaining ocean currents to me.

"And you got there?" I prompted.

"Right. We got there, and everyone jumped into the water. I pretended I was having issues with my shorts, so I told Kendra and Nathan to go ahead without me, that I'd catch up to them. Instead, I went up to talk to Matt. He was on the bridge."

"And what did you say?"

"I told him I knew it was a scam. That I spoke to Tony. Matt reassured me it wasn't. He told me he'd put his own money into this and that if there was ever a legitimate investment, it was this one. He said he trusted Tony with his life. It was all bullshit. I know it was."

"So what did you do?"

Francis shrugged, but the motion was angry. "What could I do? I told him I was getting to the bottom of this. And I told him that when I found out what was going on, I'd sue him and Tony into oblivion. I wanted my money back."

"What did Matt do?"

"He looked apologetic, but he said that I wouldn't find anything to sue over. The project was going ahead as planned, and we would all be multimillionaires. I realized there was no point in talking to him further, so I grabbed my snorkelling gear and joined my family in the water."

"Did you see anyone else on the boat when you were up there? Anything at all? Anything out of place?"

He shook his head. "No. Nothing. It was just the two of us on board."

"You're sure of that?"

"One hundred percent. I had to walk back around the whole boat to get my things when I left the bridge."

I nodded, thinking. If Francis was telling the truth—and that was a big if—it meant someone had gotten out of the water to kill Matt.

"Do you have an exact address for the development?"

"Sure. Somewhere. Look, can I text it to you, or something?" Francis glanced nervously at the water again. "My family. I don't want them…"

He trailed off, and I nodded, pulling a card from my bag and handing it to him. "Yeah, fine. When are you leaving the island?"

"Three days. But you have to believe me. I wouldn't have killed Matt. I wanted my money back more than I wanted him dead."

I nodded and left the beach, with more questions than answers. I figured that since home wasn't the safest place for me right now, I'd head over to one of the beach bars and enjoy a cocktail by the ocean.

I ordered a Maui Tai—a Mai Tai with added passion fruit juice—and sat at the bar, still pondering. Was Francis telling the truth?

I dialled Dot's number and put the phone to my ear.

"What's up?" she replied on the second ring.

"I just spoke to Francis Cooper. He's convinced Tony and Matt were running an investment scam. And one thing he said makes me think they were too."

"Oh, yeah? Matt? He was always such a nice kid, but you never really know someone, do you?"

"Well, here's the thing: Francis told me one of the selling points of the resort was that they would own the whole beach in front of it."

"Oh."

"Exactly." I knew Dot had picked up on exactly what I had. In Hawaii, almost all the beaches were open to the public by law. There were a couple of exceptions, but they were all still administered by the government. There was absolutely no way any private resort would get exclusive access to a beach in this state. None.

"Do you have an address?"

"Francis is going to send it to me."

"Do you believe him?"

I paused before answering. "I'm not sure. It's way too much of a coincidence, isn't it? Assuming he's telling the truth, of the less than twenty passengers on that boat that day, one of them just *happens* to be a guy who's screwing over one of the passengers, and that guy scamming a passenger just *happens* to get murdered by someone else, for a completely unrelated reason? It's a stretch. And Francis Cooper is definitely a liar. A good one too."

"Well, he does own six car dealerships."

"That's what I was thinking. He'd sure have experience. And like, I do believe in coincidences. They happen. Don't get me wrong. But this is almost too much. It's like believing you can train a cat to flush the toilet after it does its business."

"You can. Rosie trained Middie to do just that."

"That's just weird. And I refuse to believe it until I see it."

"I've seen it. I'll admit it's weird, though. But you know Rosie."

"Nothing should surprise me about her anymore."

"Exactly. So, you want me to look into that land?"

"Yeah. Francis said he would email me the address, just to get me out of there. Apparently, he hasn't told his wife what he did yet. He put in a million and a half."

Dot let out a low whistle. "Add this to the list of reasons I'm not married anymore. It's looking longer than a hung giraffe's dick right about how."

I spluttered, and the sip of my drink flew from my mouth and all over my shirt and the bar, earning me a glare from the bartender. I held up a hand in apology and reached over for some napkins to clean up the mess I'd just made. "Excuse me?"

"You heard me."

"Unfortunately."

"Oh, grow up."

"I'm not the one commenting on the length of giraffe dicks. You could have *very* easily said neck. Giraffe neck."

"Your reaction was much more fun this way," Dot replied, and I could practically feel her grinning through the phone.

"I'm rolling my eyes at you right now."

"I know. Prude."

"Pervert. I'll send you the address when I get it, but maybe, if you could, do a bit of digging on your own first? All I know is it's a property on the north shore, along the start of the highway that leads past Paia, with a beach fronting it that they're claiming would be private."

"I'll see what I can do."

"Thanks, Dot. You're the best."

"I know. By the way, your boy hasn't been back to his hotel room."

"Let me know when he does. I still haven't decided how I'm going to handle this, but I want to be ready."

"Will do."

I ended the call and went back to my drink. About thirty minutes later, someone slipped into the seat next to me. My hand was immediately on the Mace in my bag just in case, but the person who'd just arrived wasn't Connor Ham.

It was Kendra Cooper.

Chapter 16

"Hɪ," I sᴀɪᴅ ᴘᴏʟɪᴛᴇʟʏ ᴀs sʜᴇ ʟᴏᴏᴋᴇᴅ ᴀᴛ ᴍᴇ. "Charlie Gibson. Private investigator."

"Kendra Cooper. But you knew that already. You were speaking with Francis."

Lying to this woman would be pointless. "I was."

"You were talking to him about the dead man. The one who ripped him off."

I tried to hide my surprise, but my eyebrows still perked upward. I had half expected her to accuse me of seducing him. "You know about that?"

Kendra barked out a laugh. "He still doesn't realize it, huh? Well, that sounds about right. Francis has always been as observant as a drunk swimming in an alligator pond."

"It sounds like you don't think too much of your husband."

"He inherited ten million dollars from his father and turned it into a five-million-dollar business," Kendra said dryly. "Unfortunately, Francis is a smooth talker. Smooth enough that I fell for his whole shtick, and by the time I realized what kind of person he really was, it was too late."

"And what kind of person was that?"

"A dumbass with a trust fund, an inflated sense of self-worth, and an ego so big you can see it from space. The last one I could live with. But the rest of it? A million and a half dollars, and the idiot thinks he can hide it from me."

"How long have you known?"

"Three months. He was being more secretive than usual, and I found a slip in his desk for a deposit to a bank in Hawaii. I did some digging, and I found out about the rest of it."

"Did you know he was getting ripped off?" I asked as Kendra motioned for the bartender.

"Sure did. Mai Tai—double rum, please," she ordered, before turning back to me. "And do you know what it took? A simple Google search. Something my husband couldn't figure out how to do before spending over a million dollars on an investment scam. The promotional documents he had advertised a private beach. But there aren't any of those on Hawaii."

"That's right," I agreed.

Kendra grimaced. "Do you know what it does to you, realizing that you married a dumbass? It's the worst. Because I'm the one who married him, so what does that say about me?"

I shrugged. "You're far from the only person to make a bad decision when it comes to romance."

"You married?"

"No."

"Then you don't get it. Marriage is different. It binds you to a person. And if you add a kid into the mix, it's even worse. Sure, I could leave. But there's Nathan to think about. When you have kids, it's a whole new can of worms. Leaving, I mean. Because no matter what, he's still the father of your kid. There's still a connection, and that's going to exist at least until Nathan turns eighteen. Maybe even for the rest of his life. Divorce could only get me so far."

The bartender returned with a drink, and Kendra downed nearly the whole thing in a single gulp.

"I mean, I'm no expert, but surely being any distance from the man who makes you do that is better than the alternative," I said, motioning to the glass as Kendra put it back down on the table.

"Maybe you're right. Maybe I'm just a coward. Maybe that's why I've come here, and I still haven't asked what I want to know."

"Which is?"

"Did my husband kill that man on the boat the other day? That's why you're here, isn't it? That's what you're investigating."

"Yes." I didn't see any point in denying it. "As for whether your husband was involved, I'm not sure yet. It had to be someone on that boat. And it would be a massive coincidence if it wasn't him. Or you, for that matter."

Most people bristled when faced with the idea that they could potentially be murder suspects. They instantly got defensive. They argued. No way. How could I possibly suspect *them*?

But not Kendra.

Instead, she stared into the rest of her drink, tilted her head back, and poured it down her throat before slamming the glass onto the table again. "Babe, if I was going to murder anyone on this island, it'd be my idiot husband."

"I'll keep that in mind," I said dryly.

"You think I'm kidding, but I mean it. I don't blame Matt. Hell, good for him. He found a mark, he acted, and he came out of it with a good chunk of cash."

"You also knew it was the boat captain?"

"I do. As I said, I did some digging. Matt and the other one, Tony. They're the two men behind it, aren't they? Now, don't get me wrong. I would love for Francis to get that money back. But if he

190

doesn't? It means he just won't lose it again in another get-rich-quick investment 'scheme.'" Kendra made air quotes around the last word.

"So you bore them no ill will?"

"No."

"Well, I have to say, if you didn't kill Matt, I think it's really likely Francis did."

"Shit," Kendra muttered, staring at the glass on the table. A few drops of condensation formed on the bar surrounding her glass.

"First, help convince me you're innocent. Were you in the water the whole time?"

"Yes, with Nathan. You can't ask him, though. I don't want him involved in this. It sounds like his father has messed up badly enough this time that the kid's going to be screwed for life. I don't want to add to his therapy bills."

"Fair enough."

"He's just a kid. He didn't ask for this. Didn't ask to be born into this train wreck of a marriage. Have this kind of father."

"No, he didn't. I won't bother him."

Kendra looked at me carefully. Then, as though satisfied, she nodded. "Good. When he's arrested, please try to make sure we're not close by, either. I don't want him to see it."

"Do you think he would get violent with you?"

"If you asked me last week if I thought Francis would kill a man, I would have said no. Obviously, what I think doesn't matter, does it? I have to get back. I said I left something in the room. Francis is going to get suspicious if I take too long."

I slid a card across the table. "If you need anything, or think of anything."

Kendra shook her head. "I'll find you. Francis thinks he married a statue. Someone who was designed to stand around and look pretty, something to be admired that doesn't think for itself."

And with that, Kendra stood up from her chair and headed off. I watched as she left, her chin held high, as if she could hide that her whole life was crumbling around her if only she looked the part.

She hadn't given me much of an alibi. But then again, she'd also admitted to me that she knew all about the scheme Matt and Tony had concocted and that it was a scam. If she'd killed Matt, she could have very easily pretended not to know a thing about it. I'd have had no reason to question Francis's assertion that she didn't have a clue about what was going on, and therefore Kendra wouldn't have been so much as a blip on my radar.

But by coming here, confessing to me that she knew what her husband had done, she had opened herself up to suspicion. And when I had pointed it out, she wasn't surprised about it.

She had already figured out I'd suspect her.

Was that because she was innocent? Or was

something else going on? Kendra Cooper was a bit of an enigma. That much was certain.

But had she killed Matt?

Or had her husband?

I took a slow sip of my drink as the bartender returned.

"Have you ever seen that woman before? The one I was with?" I asked.

The man smirked. "Sure. Every day for the past week. She comes in, stands there, orders the same double-shot Mai Tai, then leaves within ten minutes. Seen her with the family too. I think she's trying to hide the drinking from them."

"Thanks." So Kendra might have a bit of a drinking problem too. Or maybe she was just overwhelmed and knew her husband didn't want his perfect wife to have a drink every once in a while.

I knew if I had her life, I'd try to sneak away for a cheeky cocktail too.

I sighed, finished off my drink, paid the bartender, then headed back out to the beach. I called Dot.

"The wife knew about the scam."

"Kendra? Are you sure?" Dot asked.

"Yeah. She told me. Came to see me. Wanted to know if her husband was a killer. I get the impression she's an extremely unhappy woman."

"Unhappy enough to murder?"

I paused, looking out over the waves lapping

against the shore before I answered. "I think she could kill, but I think if she did it, it wasn't because of the scam. I think she might have done it to frame her husband."

"Has she never heard of a divorce lawyer?"

"I don't think that'd be enough for her. I think Kendra wants Francis out of her life entirely. And I think she resents him. Massively. He thinks she's a trophy wife, and she wants him to see her as so much more than that."

"Framing him for murder successfully would do that," Dot agreed.

"Right. She says she was in the water the whole time, with her son, Nathan. She doesn't want me to talk to him, under the guise of protecting him. But I wouldn't be surprised if she's just protecting herself instead."

"What are you going to do?"

"Well, I don't think I'm going to talk to the kid. Not now. For one thing, I actually do agree with her that I don't want to traumatize it. And secondly, I don't know how to talk to kids."

"I figured that when you referred to him as 'it.'"

"They're just not my thing. But if Kendra is telling the truth, then she's right. That boy's dad probably killed someone, is going to jail, and will probably end up putting some therapist's kid through college. I don't want to add to that if I don't have to. I'm sure there are other avenues I can follow for now. If I really well and truly cannot find anything, well, then I'll consider it. But there is one other thing that's bugging me."

"Oh yeah?"

"The money. A million and a half dollars. And that's just from one investor. Matt wanted to buy stuff for his mom. Make her more comfortable. Admittedly, money doesn't get you where it used to, but three quarters of a million dollars can still get you a decent apartment on this island. Why didn't he buy a place? Where's the money?"

"I can find out for you."

"Thanks, Dot. I'd appreciate that."

"Anytime. By the way, your boy just showed back up at the resort. He looks tired."

"Good."

"Have you come up with a plan?"

"Not yet. I'm still working on it. But I'll come up with something. I have to. He's not going to leave the island until he knows I'm dead, and I don't plan on being in the ground anytime soon," I said.

"Okay. Tell me when you've figured out what you're going to do. And if you need any help. And I mean it. Anything, Charlie. We have your back."

"Is Rosie there with you now?"

"She is."

"She should be sleeping. I swear, I'm thirty,

and if I don't get at least six hours every night, I'm like a zombie the next day. Rosie isn't human."

"My mental faculties may not be quite as alert as I would like them to be, but I'm still able to function, and at this point I'd prefer to stay awake until tonight to get my circadian rhythm back into a regular routine," Rosie said.

"You're making my point for me, Robot Rosie," I told her.

"I'll call you when I have something," Dot said.

"Oh, you're not going to take a side here?" I asked.

"You wouldn't like my choice."

And then, before I had a chance to respond, Dot ended the call.

I flipped off the phone in my hand then headed back toward the car. I now knew of two people who could have killed Matt, and they both had motive. I just had to figure out which one of them did it.

As I was driving off, my phone began to ring. I threw it on speaker as I answered.

"Hey, what's up?" I asked.

To my surprise, Liam's voice came from the other end of the line. "You need to get over here. Now."

Chapter 17

I IMMEDIATELY PEELED OUT OF THE PARKING LOT and headed for Kihei Police Station. When I arrived, Liam was standing over Jake, who was sitting at his desk, a light sheen of sweat on his forehead.

"I can't deal with this boyfriend of yours anymore," Liam said when I walked in. "He's obviously out of it. He needs rest, and he won't take it."

"I don't need to rest," Jake argued, but he was obviously lying.

"You look like someone poured a can of creamed corn onto the sidewalk and left it in the sun for a few hours," I replied. "Come on. I'm taking you home. Liam can... Well, I'm sure he can look at files for a few hours."

"Hey," Liam snapped, glaring at me.

"I call 'em like I see 'em. Anyway, you were right, so thanks. He does need to rest. Come on."

"I'm fine," Jake continued to protest as I helped him up, but he let me lead him slowly toward the car. "I can find proof of the murder."

"Not in this shape, you're not. Besides, if you let yourself get overworked to the point that you collapse and die, I'm going to reverse haunt you."

"Reverse haunt me?" Jake asked with a weak chuckle.

"That's right. I'm going to spend the rest of my life only doing things that would annoy you."

"You do that now, while I'm your living, breathing boyfriend."

"Oh, you have no idea how much more annoying I can be. Ghost you will have to float around and watch while I spend every day of my life putting the glasses in the lower rack of the dishwasher. A whole lifetime of me refusing to separate my washing into whites and colors, because it's the twenty-first century and washing machines can handle doing both at once."

"You monster," Jake said, giving another weak laugh.

"That's right. So you'd best listen to me while you're alive."

"You refuse to sort your whites and colors now."

"That's true, but when I'm doing laundry at

your place, I at least pretend. If you die, I'm going to look up at you, right in your ghost eyes, while I purposely load the washing machine differently to how you do it."

"I can't believe this is what you're threatening me with."

"Oh, and don't forget, I'm also going to get into every single dangerous situation you can imagine."

"Again, you do that *now*."

"I can get so much worse."

"You were literally almost killed by the blow-hole less than twenty-four hours ago. And twelve hours before that, I had to break out of the hospital to save your life. You're not going to make it a week without me there to save you."

I puffed air out of my cheeks. "Really? Keep this up and we'll be able to test out that theory."

"I thought you were here to save me, not kill me yourself."

"Depends on how you're acting. Try not to get any blood on the seat. Olivia just cleaned the upholstery."

"Did you get shot yesterday?" Jake's eyes widened.

"No. It was shave ice."

"Do I want to ask?"

"Definitely not. But it was the ice cream or the tourist, so I think I made the right call."

"The island's tourism industry thanks you. As does the person you almost hit, I guess."

"Maybe not. Ululani's is very good shave ice."

"You have wild priorities."

Jake winced as he slid into the seat, and I looked at him with concern as I slipped behind the wheel. "You know, I'm pretty sure you're allowed to take a few days off when you've been literally shot and had a bullet dug out of your butt."

"They didn't dig it out. They left it there."

"I hope you enjoy me calling you Bullet Butt forever."

"I expect nothing less. Besides, I can't take the day off. We've already established you're incapable of staying alive without me."

"Excuse me, I was doing just fine. You might have sped things along, but I was at least ninety percent of the way there on my own."

Jake turned to me and grinned as I pressed the button that started the car. "Easy for you to say now, from the land of the living," he said.

"You're quickly ruining your odds of staying here, mister," I threatened. "Always be nice to the crazy person in charge of the steering wheel."

"That's probably good life advice," Jake replied solemnly.

I pulled back onto the highway and headed home. "Seriously, this is ridiculous. You're not going to find proof that Connor Ham is behind this. These gangsters are too good. They've been doing this back in Seattle for almost a decade now. There's a reason the cops there can't find anything on them. They know what the police look for. They cut off that dude's hands to make it harder to identify him, for God's sake."

"There's one thing they don't know," Jake mused, staring out the window, his brow furrowing as he thought.

"What's that?"

"They don't know we're together."

"Why is that important?"

"Think about it. All they took was his hands. Why?"

"To mail to the next poor, innocent person who happens to kill a Ham sibling? Although I guess that one's me again."

"No. They wanted to stop the identification for as long as possible. They figured fingerprints are in a national database, but dental records aren't. The FBI have a dental database, but it's nowhere near complete, and you basically have to be a criminal who's had work done in a prison to have your dental records on that one."

I nodded slowly as I realized what Jake was saying. "They don't realize we're together because they would have taken out his teeth if they had."

"Exactly. If they'd realized you were dating a cop, they would have known you could identify what state he came from. They would have taken his teeth too."

"So at least there's that. They've obviously done some research. They know where I live."

"But not that your policeman boyfriend lives next door."

"Right. That could make things interesting."

Jake turned and shot me a concerned look. "I don't want you doing anything stupid. You've been lucky so far. The others are dead, and it can't be traced back to you. But if you kill Connor Ham in cold blood, it's not up to me what happens. It's up to the district attorney for Maui County. And we know he's up for re-election and has been campaigning on a 'tough on crime' platform."

"I know. But I also know that Connor Ham being behind bars isn't going to be enough. Even if it's on Hawaii. I don't want to kill him. Okay, maybe a little part of me wants to kill him. A medium-sized part, even. But I won't do it in cold blood. If I'm going to kill him, it'll be in self-defense."

"Still, I don't like it. I'm scared for you, Charlie."

"And you'll still have to be scared if he's behind bars. He's not going to let go of this. I killed both his brothers, and he knows it. Even if he doesn't have proof. He'll go to the ends of the earth to kill me, even if it means destroying himself."

Jake rubbed his hands up and down his face. "I know. Deep down, I know it. But I'm a sworn officer of the law. I can't sit here and tell you I'm okay with this. Especially since I know you might not get away with it without consequences."

"Any consequence short of my death is better than the alternative if he stays alive," I said quietly.

"I worry you're right."

I cracked a smile. "On the bright side, I know that if worse comes to worst, you're willing to come out and face him down, laying everything bare."

He threw me an exasperated look. "I'm never going to hear the end of that one, either, am I?"

"Absolutely not. You're like Magnum, PI, only the PI in this case stands for 'Public Indecency.'"

"I think you can do better than that."

"Me too, but give me a break. It's only been a couple of days, and there have been multiple attempts on my life since then. How about *CSI: Full Frontal*?"

"A little better, but I expect more from you."

"That's what she said," I replied with a grin as I pulled into a visitor's spot in the parking lot, glancing at all the nearby cars to see if any looked like they didn't belong, or were obviously rentals.

The way Jake's eyes scanned the lot told me he was doing the same thing.

"What are your plans now?" Jake asked. "After you get my infirm ass to bed, where I will continue to research this case from my phone?"

"I'm this close to solving Matt's murder. It was someone he scammed, or the wife. I'm actually thinking I might go speak to his best friend, who works in construction. He might know something that could help."

"It's crazy to think this murder case is somehow the less dangerous thing you're involved in right now."

"Don't you love being in a relationship with me?"

"I do," Jake replied, his eyes filling with warmth as he gazed at me. "Even though I know you're going to be the death of me somehow. Either physically, or mentally."

"Half the fun is keeping you on your toes."

"Just wait until I'm back to one hundred percent," he replied with a cheeky grin.

The two of us headed upstairs, slowly, and Jake unlocked the door. I helped him settle into bed, got him some water for the nightstand, and watched as his cat, Miss Butters, curled up in the crook between his knees. She made a couple of biscuits against his hamstrings before curling up into a ball and resting her head on his leg.

"You'd better not leave here until at least tomorrow," I warned.

"I won't," Jake promised. I was only about thirty percent sure he was telling the truth, but I felt a lot more positive about it when I went out into the bathroom, grabbed some of the pain drugs he'd been prescribed, and came back to find him already fast asleep.

I smiled as I watched his slow, steady breath, placed the pills on the table next to him, and carefully headed out. I had a killer to find.

MATT'S BEST FRIEND, KONANE, WORKED AT A construction site in Kihei, exactly where Andi told me I'd find him. I pulled up to the site, where another luxury home was being built, and tried to push out the thoughts of what I'd found the last time I was on a similar lot.

Here, however, the site was far from abandoned. At least fifty men worked in the blazing heat of the Maui day, and when I arrived, a security guard approached the car, taking down my license plate number and asking for my details.

I gave them to him, and the guard motioned for me to park back out onto the street.

When I returned, a man walked toward me. In his late twenties, Konane had deeply tanned skin from working in the sun all day and black tribal tattoos running up and down his arms. His form-fitting gray T-shirt was stained with paint, grease, and other random construction site dirt, and despite the warmth of the day, he still had on a pair of jeans. Steel-toed boots and a white hard hat over a pair of plain sunglasses completed the look. He removed the hard hat as he held out a hand.

"Konane Makali. Andi called me last night. She told me you're looking for the person who killed Matt."

Konane spoke confidently, but his voice wavered slightly as he said those last two words.

"I am. Thanks for speaking with me."

"Of course. But there's no need to waste time. I can tell you who did it. That asshole, Tony."

Chapter 18

THAT WAS QUICK. "TONY BRADLEY? MATT'S business partner?"

Konane motioned for me to follow him, and we exited the construction site, the din behind us steadily quieting as we walked along the residential street, the sounds of nail guns and saws quickly replaced with the songs of birds, *keiki* playing in the street, and dogs barking.

"He's the one," Konane said, staring at the ground when we were about a hundred feet from the site. "I know it down to my core. Slimy motherfucker. He was a scammer, you know?"

"I did know that," I replied, choosing my words carefully. I wanted Konane to tell me what he knew without being influenced by my own thoughts—namely, that Matt himself was also involved in scamming people.

"He wasn't just scamming customers. He scammed Matt too. And Matt finally figured it out."

"Oh?" This was new.

Konane bobbed his head up and down quickly, his hands curling into fists. The tips of his knuckles went white; this was an angry man. "Matt found out about it only a few days before he died."

"Can you tell me everything from the start? What did Matt tell you?"

"He ran into Tony because the two worked near each other. Tony was trying to lease out the office above the main Zodiac Cruises shop. They'd meet in line for coffee at one of the shops near the harbor in the morning. They became friends, and eventually Tony suggested they go into business together on a new development on the north side of the island. Matt had access to affluent customers through the business. People from the island who didn't know any better. And Tony had the slick salesman pitch down. Between the two of them, they'd get a bunch of suckers who didn't know any better to invest in a fake product, and they'd both rake it in."

Konane glanced at me out of the corner of his eye, and I held up my hands. "I already knew. Don't worry, I'm not judging."

"I'm not sure what I thought about it," Konane admitted, kicking at the ground as we continued. "On the one hand, Matt assured me he was only roping in assholes. You know, the kind of people who refuse to use the reef-safe sunscreen that doesn't kill the marine life around here. The ones who don't tip. Who feel entitled to everything because they have a bit of money. Do I feel bad for those people? No. But my parents raised me to know right from wrong, and knowingly scamming people? Doesn't really matter how scummy they are. That's still a shit thing to do. But Matt wasn't having it."

"He justified it to himself?" I asked quietly.

Konane looked sadly down at his hands. "He did. It didn't matter what I said. He told me he'd earned this. It was his chance to get out. To make something for his mom. He always wanted her to have the best, but we both knew that wasn't going to happen while he was piloting that boat. He made a living, sure, but that was about it. And you know, with inflation these days, even that doesn't really get you as far as it used to."

I nodded. "Yeah. I get it."

"Matt saw the scam as his way out. Yeah, he knew he was ripping people off. But he told himself it was people who deserved to be separated from their money. Fools and all that."

"He never expected it to happen to him, though?"

Konane shook his head. "Nope. He thought he

and Tony were in it together. I warned him. I told him, a guy like that, willing to steal from *haoles*, he'd steal from him too. But Matt wouldn't listen. He was convinced I was wrong. He thought he and Tony were ride or die."

"Until they weren't. How did Matt find out he was getting ripped off?"

"He ran into one of their marks the other day. Some dude from the Midwest. That doesn't really narrow it down, does it? I think that's where most of the people they were scamming come from. Anyway, Matt starts talking to him and quickly realizes the guy's figured it all out. He knows it's a scam. But then he tells Matt he invested one and a half mil."

"And Matt realizes Tony's told him it's less," I said with an understanding nod.

"Exactly right. Matt called me right after he left the guy. Told me what had happened. I could hear over the phone how angry he was. He told me he was going right over to see Tony. Wasn't giving him a heads-up. He wanted him to tell him straight up he know what was going on."

"How much did Matt get paid? Do you know?"

"Half a million. Tony told him they'd taken the guy for a million bucks. Turns out it was a million and a half."

"Do you know the name of the guy in question?"

"No. Matt didn't tell me, and I didn't ask."

Given the figures mentioned and the timeline, I thought it was still safe to assume Francis Cooper was the man Matt had encountered.

I motioned for Konane to keep talking. "So, Matt went and spoke to Tony?"

"I offered to go with him if he wanted, but Matt refused. He said he was going to take care of this on his own. He called me a couple hours later, wanted to go out for a drink. I met him at the bar, and he was already a few beers in. He said Tony screwed him over and wouldn't admit to it. He didn't know what to do but was going to get his revenge on Tony."

"What was he going to do? It's not like he could sue him. You don't use the courts to settle your illegal scam disputes."

"I know. That was my first thought too. But I think Matt was just ranting. He hadn't actually thought it through. He would have never actually hurt Tony. He just wanted his share of the money."

"What did Tony say when Matt confronted him?"

"Obviously, I've only got one side of the story. Matt told me Tony tried to initially play it off as some sort of misunderstanding. Like the other guy was confused. But Matt continued to press, and eventually Tony admitted what he'd done. Said he never intended to hurt Matt, blah blah blah, that he would make it right. You know, normal lies."

"Did Matt threaten Tony?"

Konane hoisted a single shoulder skyward. "Don't know. He said he didn't. Do I believe him? I don't know. What I do know is Matt wouldn't have actually *done* anything. He wasn't a violent person. He was just a little bit greedy, and he got in with the wrong guy. But Tony? Yeah, I totally believe he would have killed Matt. Look at the dude. He was ripping off people left, right, and center, and it finally came back to haunt him."

"Only one problem with that: Tony wasn't on the boat that morning, and whoever killed Matt had to be."

Konane shook his head. "Nah. I don't believe that. Tony would have killed Matt."

"The man who he spoke to the other day was on the boat. With his family. He's currently at the top of the suspect list."

He let out a low whistle. "Damn. Matt really got himself in too deep. This is why I told him not to do it. He wanted cash, but he wasn't a bad person. Deep down, I mean. He got too greedy, but he wasn't a psycho. Not like some of these other people. He wouldn't have killed. He just got himself killed. And he didn't deserve it."

"I'm sorry."

"Thanks. It hurts, but at the same time, Matt kind of brought this on himself. He offered to bring me into it, you know? Right at the beginning. I turned him down. And sure, when Matt said he had a half mil in the bank, I might have regretted saying no a little bit. Who wouldn't? But it wasn't me. I knew that. I wasn't going to be that person. And Matt wasn't that person either. He just couldn't see it. He was swimming with sharks, but he thought he was one of them. He didn't realize he was chum."

"Did he tell you anything about the investor that might help me prove that he killed Matt? Maybe that man threatened him?"

Konane shook his head again. "We didn't really talk about him that much. It was more about Tony. And it has to be him, doesn't it? That guy, he knew Matt was getting screwed over too. Tony, on the other hand, was feeling it from both sides. From Matt and from the victim. He probably thought getting rid of Matt was his safest bet. It would stop Matt from going after him for his share of the extra half mil, and it would send a message to the other guy, right? Especially if they were on the same boat."

I pursed my lips. "You might be right, but it's still impossible. Tony wasn't one of the customers on that boat. He couldn't have done it. He would have been recognized if he'd been on it, even under a fake name. Andi met Tony, too, he said."

Konane ran a hand through his hair. "Yeah, she did. I know Matt introduced them. Then I guess it was the customer who lost his money. Damn. This is why I didn't want Matt involved. It never ends well, this sort of thing. Someone always gets hurt. I just wish it had been Tony and not my best friend."

"And nothing else was going on in Matt's life that could have led to this?"

"Definitely not."

"How was his relationship with Andi?"

The corners of Konane's mouth curled up into a smile. "Great. They were happy. He was going to propose to her, you know? He was looking for the right ring. He wanted something surrounded by sapphires. It was her birthstone, and it would represent the ocean."

"So there was nothing going on in their relationship, as far as you know?"

Konane stopped, and I paused as he looked at me carefully. "No. Believe me, Matt would have told me if there was something wrong. I know, you probably hear that a lot. But Matt and me, we're closer than brothers. Andi loved him too. I saw her with him. You could tell. They were soulmates. I don't for a second believe she would have had anything to do with this. Trust me."

"Okay."

"I know you don't think it was Tony. But he had the most to lose here. I don't know how he did it. But you have to believe me, it was him."

"All right. Thanks for the help."

"Yeah. I just wish I could help more. You didn't know him, did you?"

I shook my head.

Konane continued, "And so you didn't know what a good guy he really was. I know you probably think he was a scumbag, and I can't blame you, finding out what you did about him. But he really was more than just a scammer. Deep down, Matt was a decent person. He just had this one flaw, that he wanted money more than anything in the world. And that cost him his life. It shouldn't have. It was a steep price to pay for the one vice he had."

He bit his bottom lip; I knew he was hurting right now. His friend was dead, and he felt helpless to do anything about it. I knew the feeling.

"It'll get better," I said quietly. "But it's going to take a long time."

"I know," Konane whispered. "And it fucking sucks. But you know what? I want you to nail Tony to the wall for this. Or whoever did it, if it really wasn't him. You have to find who did this. Please. Matt deserves that, at the very least."

"I'll do my best," I promised.

Konane nodded. "What's your number? In case I think of anything else."

I gave Konane a card and said goodbye to him and headed back to Queenie, biting my inner lip as I considered what he said. He was right: Tony did have excellent motive to kill Matt. But it was impossible. He simply couldn't have done it.

I scrolled through the text messages I'd received from Dot and found the information for Calvin, the former Maui resident who had also been on that boat. I figured it couldn't hurt to pay him a visit. I had no proof right now that Francis or Kendra Cooper had killed Matt, and that was what I needed. Proof. Maybe Calvin would be able to help shine some light on it.

Chapter 19

He was staying at a nearby vacation rental. I drove to the address, parked in a visitor's spot, and took the elevator up to the residential building's fourth floor. Reaching door 412, I knocked, and about twenty seconds, later a man answered.

Standing a smidgen under six feet tall, Calvin was the shade of a cooked lobster. Evidently, moving away from Maui and then returning had made him forget what the sun could do to a person. He stood in front of me, wearing only board shorts, a bit of paunch sliding over the waist of his elastic.

"Yes?" he asked, looking me up and down with idle curiosity.

"Calvin?"

"That's me."

"I'm Charlie Gibson, a private investigator looking into Matt Hogan's death."

"Who?"

"The captain of the boat you were on the other day."

"Oh, right. That guy."

Nothing about Calvin's tone or body language implied that he gave the slightest of shits about Matt.

"Did you know him when you lived on the island?"

Calvin's expression turned to one of suspicion. "How do you know I used to live here?"

"It's my job. Someone murdered Matt. I'm looking into everyone who was on that boat."

"Yeah, well, I didn't have anything to do with that."

"Cool, then help me figure out who did and I'll be out of your hair sooner than you know."

"Why are you looking at me, anyway?"

"Because I'm looking at everyone. Did you know Matt when you lived on the island?"

"No. Never met him before in my life before that day."

"Are you sure?"

"Yes. And anyone who says otherwise is lying." He crossed his arms across his chest as he leaned against the doorway. "Didn't know him. Didn't have nothing against him. Didn't kill him. Don't know who did."

"What about the other passengers on the boat? Did you see any of them talking to him?"

Calvin frowned. "Yeah, sure. There was one guy. On the way over, he kept going up to the bridge and talking to the guy. It didn't look like they were having a nice little chat, if you know what I mean."

"They were fighting," I stated.

"I can't say for sure. Couldn't hear them. But if I were a betting man, that's what I'd say."

"This the guy you saw?" I asked, pulling out my phone and opening a photo of Francis Cooper.

Calvin leaned down to squint at the screen then drew himself back up to his full height as he nodded. "That's the one."

"Did you notice who he was with?"

"His wife. And a kid, I think. The wife saw him chatting with the dead guy. She kept glaring at him. I got the feeling she wasn't thrilled with him."

"Did you see them later? In the water, I mean?"

Calvin pursed his lips as he thought about his answer. "I think so. Yeah. I saw her, for sure. She was with the kid. He kept asking her to find him a shark. She told him they could swim near the reef but that if the sharks didn't want to come out and say hi, he had to respect that."

"You're one hundred percent sure it was them?"

"Positive. I remember thinking that there was no way that marriage was going to last with that dude, since he wasn't even with his family."

"When was this, exactly?"

Calvin shrugged. "I don't know. Five, maybe ten minutes after we all left the boat to go snorkelling? I wasn't exactly paying that much attention to them. I was trying to find an eel for Sara, my girlfriend."

"And did you?"

Calvin grinned. "Showed her the one in my pants when we got back on shore."

I didn't bother hiding my eye roll. "Congratulations," I said dryly.

"Thank you." Calvin obviously didn't catch the sarcasm dripping from my voice.

"Did you see any of them at any other time? Or notice anything happening on the boat while you were in the water? It doesn't matter how important or unimportant you think it could be."

Calvin shrugged. "Don't think so. Not really. It was just a normal tour until someone screamed, and then it all turned to chaos. We weren't allowed back on the boat. We had to go to shore. One of the workers, she was really upset."

I nodded. That would have been Andi. "Did anything strange happen once you got to shore?"

"I don't think so. Not that I noticed. Guy was dead at that point, right? What else could have happened?"

"Okay, thanks." I handed him a card. "Let me know if you think of anything else, okay?"

"Yeah. But, like, I don't know anything. I'm just here with my girlfriend for a week before we go back home."

"Not getting into any bar fights or anything these days?"

Calvin scowled. "That was a misunderstanding."

"I'm not judging."

"You sound like you're judging."

"Only if you killed the captain."

"I already told you I didn't."

"Then you have nothing to worry about, do you?"

I left Calvin, and he slammed the door shut behind me. Was he annoying? Yes. But as far as I could tell, nothing he said made me think he was the killer. If anything, he had confirmed what both Francis and Kendra Cooper had told me.

It didn't make it impossible that they were the killers. In fact, I still suspected them more than anyone.

But at the same time, what if it wasn't either of them?

Suddenly, it hit me.

I practically sprinted back down to Rosie's car. Then I slammed it into gear and I sped off back toward the harbour.

As soon as I arrived, I parked and looked around.

Reggie was just emerging from the harbour, and I ran toward him.

"Reggie!"

He looked up and around, and as soon as he spotted me, he lifted his hand and waved. "Charlie. What do you need?"

"A tour of that boat. Can you give me ten minutes? It's important."

He tilted his head slightly to one side. "This one? Sure. But it's not the boat that Matt took out. The police have that one."

"I know. But the other day, when I interviewed you, you said the two catamarans were identical, right?"

"Sure. The owner bought them at the same time. Exact same model."

"Great. That's all I need. I don't need *the* boat Matt was on. I just need to see one like it. Can you do it?"

Reggie looked out toward the storefront. A few people were walking in, happy-looking customers who had obviously enjoyed their ocean cruise. "Sure. I guess so, if it'll help. Why not? Come on."

I followed him onto the wooden dock, which bobbed ever so slightly up and down in the water with the movement of our bodies, the water gasping against it as it hit the wood.

Reggie led me out to a medium-sized cata-maran docked about halfway along. Thick ropes expertly tied it to the dock, and she gleamed white with the company logo emblazoned in blue along the side.

"Did you and Matt ever switch boats?" I asked, looking at the vessel carefully. "Or did you always take the same one?"

"Depends on the day. The schedule is always written on the board in the office."

"In the public area, or in the back, in private?"

"Both."

Reggie jumped deftly onto the deck and then reached over, offering me a hand. I jumped across, much less deftly, grabbing onto the exterior rail as if for dear life before hoisting a leg over the railing and flopping onto the deck with an elegance a manatee would have been embarrassed about.

If he'd noticed—and I was sure he'd noticed—Reggie didn't point out my lack of co-ordination, fortunately. I didn't like the ocean, and that included boats. They moved too much.

"This is her," he said, motioning across the

deck as I stood up. We were on the main stretch, with the front of the ship to the left and the back to the right. "This is where our customers come on board."

Reggie began walking toward the back of the boat, and I followed him down the narrow space to a large rear deck. Two small staircases led from either side of the deck and down to the water level.

The back of the deck led to a covered space. I walked into it; on either side stood a table, and long, pillowed benches lined three sides around them.

"This is where we guide customers right away. They can leave all of their gear they've brought on board safely; if anything weird happens when we're on the water, it can't fly over the edge."

Directly in front of me was a door, just behind one of the benches. "What's that?" I asked.

"Storage. It's where we keep extra life vests, food, drinks, and anything the crew wants."

"Can you open it for me?"

Reggie shrugged. "Sure."

He walked over and yanked on the door handle, which opened the storage space.

"Do you ever keep it locked?" I asked as I stepped up to the doorway and looked inside. It was roomier than I thought in there. Sure enough, there were a few 24-packs of Coke and Sprite, some bright orange life jackets, and, at the back, a pile of old blankets.

"Sometimes. If anyone has anything especially secure they want to keep on board. But for the most part, we leave it open. It's not like anyone goes in there except us, and there's never anything valuable in there. If someone is that desperate for an extra can of Coke, who am I to say no to that?"

"Does someone go in there every day?"

"Nah," Reggie said, shaking his head. "Only if it's fully necessary. Why?"

I ignored his question; the wheels in my head were turning. I thought I knew now who had killed Matt. And why.

Just when I was about to tell Reggie we could leave and getting ready to pull out my phone to call Jake, I heard the cocking of a gun behind me.

"You move, you die."

I spun around to see Tony behind us on the deck, pointing a pistol directly at me.

Chapter 20

R<small>EGGIE</small> <small>IMMEDIATELY</small> <small>THREW</small> <small>HIS</small> <small>HANDS</small> <small>UP.</small> "Whoa, whoa. Easy there, dude. There's no need to do anything rash. What's going on?"

"She figured it out. That's what's going on," Tony replied. "And I can't let her get away with this. You, get in," he ordered, motioning with the gun for me to get into the hole.

Realizing it was either crawl into the creepy, dark hole that suddenly looked a lot smaller than I first thought, or get shot, I did as he ordered.

"And throw me your phone," he ordered. Damn. "You too."

I carefully reached into my bag and pulled my phone out, leaving it on the bench in front of me while Reggie placed his own phone on the table.

"You're going in here. You, you're going to drive this boat," Tony ordered.

He strode across the small cabin in a few steps and shoved me inside, slamming the door shut behind me. I let out a small gasp of surprise as the light of the day immediately disappeared and I found myself in complete darkness.

I paused for a couple of moments, letting my heart rate settle from the shock of having solved the crime and almost immediately afterward having Tony confront me and lock me in this storage space.

The same storage space where he had concealed himself before the boat left that morning, to hide that he was going to kill Matt.

About a minute later, the engine began to hum, and the floor beneath me vibrated gently. Then, I was pushed slightly off-balance; we were moving. Tony was forcing Reggie to drive the boat out onto the ocean. Where he would undoubtedly frame Reggie for my own death. I was sure Tony's plan involved neither one of us coming out of this alive.

I quickly set about making sure that didn't happen. I immediately turned on the light on my watch. It didn't exactly light up the space, but it gave me just enough illumination that I could make my way around. I pulled the watch off my wrist and held it in front of me as I looked at the latch on the door. Getting out of this storage space was my first concern.

Luckily, being best friends with Rosie meant mandatory training in certain skills that could come in handy in my line of work. Such as picking locks. I used a combination of the light and the feeling in my fingers to find the other side of the latch. How easy was it going to be to break out of here from this side?

I had a careful look at the latch—as much as I could, anyway, with my eyesight powered entirely by Apple Watch—and breathed a sigh of relief. This was one of those locks that could be easily popped open from inside.

I pressed the back of my finger against the button and felt a small click. It was no more difficult than unlocking an interior door inside a home.

Grinning to myself, because there was no way I was letting a guy like Tony get away with this crime, I climbed out of the storage space and carefully checked my surroundings. No sign of him. Not a surprise; he would likely be up on the bridge with Reggie, trying to find the perfect place to dump my body.

He wouldn't be the first guy to try to fail at that particular task this week.

Steeling myself, I carefully crept out from the interior cabin and shot a glance upward, toward the bridge.

Sure enough, Tony was standing there, his legs

spread apart like he was trying to do his best impression of a pro wrestler, his gun levelled at Reggie. Tony's back was to me, the sound of the wind and the boat's engine covering any noise that might have betrayed my escape.

I looked around for something, anything that might help stop him without allowing him to see me. My eyes landed on the emergency life preserver hanging on the side of the boat. There was probably a law in Hawaii that required boats to have one, and in this case, I *was* going to use it to save a life.

Just not the life of someone currently in the water.

I plucked the life preserver up the wall and carefully began creeping toward the steps on the side of the boat that led to the bridge. I climbed them one by one, the life preserver in front of me, careful to watch Tony.

If he turned around, at this point, it was over.

I crept ever closer, but it was obvious he wouldn't hear me coming.

Finally, when I was about ten feet away, I pounced.

Sprinting toward him, I threw the life preserver over his shoulders and slammed it down as hard as I could.

Tony let out a cry of surprise, and the gun

clattered to the floor, sliding across the deck of the boat and falling off the ledge.

I pressed the life preserver down over Tony's shoulders and quickly darted away as he turned toward me, his arms trapped.

"You bitch," he snarled as he ran toward me.

"Come on, buddy, this is basically a scene out of *Monty Python and the Holy Grail*," I quipped as I took a quick step to the right as he ran at me. Predictably, Tony hit the railing on the ledge and, unable to stop himself with his arms, toppled over the side of it, his legs flying upward as he spun through the air and flipped over and over.

"Reggie," I shouted, and he turned to look at me, surprise registering on his face.

I motioned for him to cut the engine, and he did. Then I raced toward the edge of the boat to see what had happened to Tony.

He was floating in the water, bobbing up and down, spluttering away while the hair that he'd gelled back so carefully was splattered across his forehead.

"Help!" he shouted, struggling in the water. "Help me!"

"Hey, look, a talking buoy," I said to Reggie with a grin.

Reggie's eyes widened as he took in the scene. "Should we, uh, help him?"

"I guess so. But give me a minute."

I pulled out my phone and turned on the video recorder. "Hey, Tony, tell me you killed Matt, and I'll let you back onto the boat."

"Save me, you bitch," he shouted back.

"That's no way to speak to a woman who's this close to the engine's throttle," I shouted back. "Now, do you want to spend the rest of your life in prison, or do you want to spend it bobbing away here in the water? Because those are your two options."

For a minute, I thought Tony was going to take the latter.

"I'm drowning," he called out.

"Not fast enough," I shouted back.

"You have to save me! You wouldn't leave me here!"

"You have no idea how many people lost that bet before. Are you sure you want to see if I'm bluffing?"

Next to me, Reggie was starting to look concerned. "Are... are you sure this is the right thing to do? He looks like he's in real trouble."

"It's fine. Besides, he tried to kill us."

"I know. But just because he's a killer doesn't mean I'll be one."

"I promise, if that asshole goes under, I'll go rescue him myself. And I hate the water." I raised my voice. "Time's running out, Tony. Are you going to become part of the Great Pacific

Garbage Patch, or are you going to tell me the truth?"

"Fine," he finally shouted. "Fine, I'll tell you. I killed Matt. I snuck onto the boat and hid in the storage locker, and when everyone else was gone, I came out and stabbed him. Then I swam to shore, walked to town, and hitched a ride onto the ferry from there—when my clothes were dry, so no one would ever know."

"Now, that wasn't so hard, was it? And you tried to kill us because you realized I had figured it all out."

"I saw you walking toward the boat, and I knew what you'd realized. You walked with purpose. Someone who had solved the case. I couldn't let that happen. I can't go to jail. I just can't."

"I mean, I can leave you in the water," I suggested.

"No," Tony shrieked. He began moving his body back and forth in the water, trying to stay upright. He looked like a freshly caught salmon flopping around on the deck of the boat.

"Fine. But it's jail for you."

Reggie steered the boat slowly toward Tony and grabbed him, while I picked up the gun that had slid across the deck and tucked it into my waistband, just to be safe. Eventually, with the help of some of the equipment on board, Reggie helped a spluttering, coughing Tony onto the deck and removed the life preserver that had been wedged onto his whole body.

He threw up about half an ocean's worth of seawater onto the deck. When he was finished, he gasped for air, on all fours, before looking up and glaring at me.

"You," he snarled. "This is your fault."

"You started it," I shot back. "You killed Matt. You came onto the boat. You tried to kill me. You're lucky I didn't leave you out there."

Tony shuddered at the thought. "You were supposed to think it was Francis."

"I know. But unlike you, I'm not always looking for the easy way out. Like scamming people from the Midwest into a property that doesn't exist. I do the work. And that's how I figured out it was you."

"How did he do it?" Reggie asked.

I looked over at Tony and smiled sweetly. "Do you want to tell him, or can I do it for you?"

Tony responded by flipping me the bird.

I shrugged. "I guess that's my invitation. Do correct me if I get any of this wrong, Tony, but I don't think I have. Tony and Matt were involved in a real estate scheme together, one that involved ripping off tourists in a fake investment scam. It was all going well until two things happened: one of their targets figured out what they were doing and was starting to kick up a fuss, and Matt found out through him that Tony was ripping him off too. Tony was getting it from both ends and figured, 'Why not kill two birds with one knife?' He found out Francis Cooper and his family were going on a snorkelling trip with Matt, where Francis was undoubtedly going to confront him. I'm assuming Francis told him about it?"

Tony shook his head, still looking at the floor. "Matt did," he said, his voice hoarse. "He saw Francis and his family on the list of upcoming tours a few days ahead of time and asked me if there was anything he should do to protect himself."

I turned back to Reggie. "There you have it. I'm wondering if that didn't give Tony the idea. Francis wanting to hurt Matt. Now, all he had to do was make it happen. Tony hid in the boat's storage container. He would have gone onto the boat early, so no one would have noticed him. The boat left the harbour with all the passengers on board, and Tony waited until it arrived at its destination. When everyone left, he finally emerged. He waited for Matt to be alone on the boat—maybe he even saw Francis talking to him before —and stabbed him. Then, the job done, Tony jumped from the boat and swam to shore. Stanford swim team, right?"

This time, Tony just glowered at me.

Reggie ran a hand through his hair. "I can't believe it. You killed him. You killed Matt. And for what? Some scam you had going?"

"That's exactly it," I confirmed.

"Okay, you watch him. I'm going to take this boat back to the harbour. I'll make sure the police are waiting when we get there."

Tony moved his hand around, as if looking for the gun.

"Sorry, buddy. This one's all mine," I said, pulling it from my waistband and dangling it in front of him. "You're cooked. Just be glad you got out of this with your life."

"I'll make you pay for this, you bitch," Tony snarled before coughing up another lungful of seawater.

"Yeah, I've heard that one before."

Chapter 21

SURE ENOUGH, BY THE TIME WE REACHED THE shore, the police were already parked at the harbour, and I delivered him right to them in silver handcuffs. Well, okay, they put the handcuffs on him, but the play on words was right there.

Reggie stood next to me as I watched the officers take Tony away, while he shouted his innocence in vain at any passersby willing to listen.

The police certainly weren't in any mood to entertain him.

"I still can't believe he did it," Reggie said, his voice hollow. "You know, he tried to get me in on his scam too."

"Did he?" I asked, turning toward him.

Reggie swallowed hard. "About six months ago. He didn't pitch it as a scam then. A legitimate business arrangement we'd be partners in. I could find investors on the boat. He would finish the sales."

"Why didn't you do it?" I asked, squinting as I shielded my face against the sun's late-afternoon rays to look at Reggie.

"My Spidey senses started tingling. Something about it felt off. He promised I'd make a ton of money, and I mean, maybe I'm just a jaded millennial, but that's not a thing that happens. Not legitimately."

"You were smart to stay out of it. Matt didn't make the same choice."

"I easily could have. I could have used the money. And I know Matt wouldn't have spent what he got on himself. He wanted money for his mom. Wanted her to live a lifestyle she deserved. I wish he'd understood that she would have lived in a tent on the beach if it meant watching her son grow up."

The two of us watched in silence as one of the police officers opened the door and stepped into the cruiser then pulled out of the harbour. Tony sat in the back, leaning forward, obviously arguing with the cops.

I had no doubt Reggie was right.

When I got back into the car, I called Dot and Rosie. "I'm coming over. The man who killed Matt has just been arrested."

"Good work," Rosie said.

"What's Connor Ham up to?" I asked. "Any update on him?"

"He went back to his hotel room for about ten minutes at one point and then left again. I think you need to assume the worst here, Charlie," Dot replied.

"Okay. Well, I'm coming over. And he's the only focus now. This has to end. And it has to end fast."

I headed over to Dot's place, and as soon as I entered, Middie rubbed herself up against my legs and purred gently.

"It's a trap," Dot said, glaring at the cat.

"Is the honeymoon period over, then?" I asked with a small smile.

"Do you know what this creature did an hour ago? She climbed up onto the windowsill and began eating poor old Larry."

"I'm sure I'm going to regret asking this, but who's Larry?"

"My succulent," Dot replied, as if it were the most normal thing in the world. "And she ate him! Then she knocked him down onto the floor."

"I mean, I feel like all of this is very normal cat behavior."

"That's what I said," Rosie replied.

"This is why I've never had cats," Dot muttered.

"She can hear you, you know?" Rosie said, leaning down and covering Middie's ears as she sent Dot a withering glare.

I smiled to myself. This was the most mothering I'd ever seen Rosie do.

"Don't tell me the two of you are having a lovers' quarrel," I teased.

"A quarrel? This? Don't be ridiculous," Dot replied.

"We don't *quarrel*," Rosie added, shooting me a look. "We're simply discussing the merits of Middie choosing to spend some of her time in this house so she can be with me."

"I thought you trained her."

"Yes, to steal things. And… some other things. I haven't trained her not to eat succulents."

"Maybe you should focus on that," Dot muttered under her breath.

"This is like watching your parents fight," I said with a small smile.

Both Rosie and Dot turned their ire onto me.

"Keep that up and you'll find out what else Rosie has been teaching that cat," Dot said. "It involves the claws."

"She's not lying," Rosie added.

I held up my hands in surrender. "All right, all right, I take it all back."

"Good," Dot said. "What are your plans for the rest of the night? We have to figure something out about Connor."

I sighed. "It's going to have to wait until the morning. I have dinner with my mom and her new boyfriend. On the bright side, I managed to convince her to let Zoe and Henry come too."

"You know, you could just be an adult and go yourself," Rosie pointed out.

I scrunched up my face. "Do you know how awkward it's going to be?"

"You actually think it's going to be less awkward if you somehow also bring your best friend and her boyfriend?" Dot asked, raising her eyebrows.

"Mom has always liked Zoe. She's basically the daughter she wishes I was. So it's kind of like Zoe's her daughter too."

"That's such a big stretch I think my muscles just snapped listening to that," Rosie replied, looking unimpressed.

"It'll be fine," I insisted. "Besides, I don't trust the guy."

"Why, because he's dating your mother?" Dot asked.

"Exactly."

"And what's wrong with that?" Rosie asked.

I waved my hands in the air. "It's just sketchy, okay?"

"You know what? I take it back. It's a good thing Zoe and Henry are coming to your dinner, because you need someone, literally anyone else around for your mom and this man to talk to."

"See?" I replied, crossing my arms. "I knew what I was doing."

"Yes, you're obviously handling this with a level of maturity I would expect of a woman of your age," Rosie said dryly.

"Look on the bright side. Connor might find me tonight before I have to have dinner with my mom, while she introduces me to a man she's been dating and hid from me because she was afraid I'd freak out."

"And do something weird like invite your best friend to be a double date?" Dot asked.

"You're not going to shut up about that, are you? It's not *that* weird."

"It's that weird, and sad," Rosie confirmed.

"All right, well, in that case, I will leave you to fight over whether or not Middie is allowed to eat succulents, because I have a very normal dinner to get to. I'll call you after I'm done, and we're going to end this once and for all."

"Keep your back to the wall, and face the entrances," Rosie ordered. "Where are you eating?"

"Monkeypod."

"Try and get an indoor table. Make sure it's not an open space. You don't want to make yourself a target. We'll keep an eye on Connor, but it takes only a second for someone like him to strike."

I swallowed hard. "Got it."

"And Charlie?" Dot said.

"Yeah?"

"Good luck."

"Do you mean about Connor?"

"No, I mean about not putting your foot in your mouth at some point tonight."

I glared at her as I headed for the door. "That's not going to happen."

LOOKING AT THE TIME, I HAD TO HEAD STRAIGHT from Dot's place to the restaurant where Mom and I were meeting. Lucas Aoki was a contract lawyer on the island and, based on what I gathered by asking around, a well-respected one at that. He'd never been involved in anything shady, he didn't have a criminal record, and as far as lawyers went, people seemed to actually like him.

There seemed to be nothing wrong with him. And I had to admit, I had come to terms with Mom dating again. She didn't have to live like a nun the rest of her life just because Dad died. I might have been a little bit on edge at first, but I made my peace with it.

Mom was dating. By all accounts, he was a nice guy. There was no reason for me not to trust him, and I wasn't going to let the fact that I wasn't exactly great with change spoil this relationship for Mom.

She deserved to be happy, first and foremost.

We were eating at Monkeypod in Wailea, which Lucas had chosen, and which I had to admit reluctantly was one of my favorite restaurants on the island. His decision of venue was certainly a point in his favor.

I parked Rosie's car in the mall parking lot and spotted Zoe and Henry heading toward the restaurant, hand in hand.

Jumping out, I called out to them and waved. They stopped and waited as I headed toward them.

"Thanks for coming," I said, slightly breathlessly, when I reached them. "I've been told that inviting you to this dinner is kind of weird, so I appreciate you going along with it."

Zoe laughed good-naturedly. "Honestly, on the list of weird things that have happened to me because of you, this doesn't even crack the top hundred."

"It probably doesn't make my top ten, and I've

known you for less than a year," Henry added with a wink. Henry Iosua was the owner of Clean Marine Hawaii, a tech start-up dedicated to cleaning the world's oceans. We met during a previous investigation, when one of his employees turned out to be a killer. I had invited him to our apartment complex's Christmas party, where he met Zoe, and the two of them clicked immediately. They'd been dating ever since.

"Well, good," I replied, not knowing what else to say. "But seriously, thank you for coming."

"Of course," Zoe said, a small smile creeping up her face. "And I promise not to tell either one of them about how you stalked them to find out this was happening."

"It wasn't *stalking*," I scowled.

"It was definitely stalking."

The three of us walked up to the hostess at the front of the stairs leading to the restaurant and announced our arrival for our reservation. She led us up the stairs and into the building.

Monkeypod Kitchen was gorgeous, airy and light, with high ceilings, plenty of pale wood, and tropical prints on the backs of the chairs. The huge windows were left open wide to let in as much natural light as possible. Two semicircular booths in the middle cut through the space, giving it more personality than if there were just tables and chairs set up in a plain rectangle.

The hostess directed us toward a six-person table against the wall, and I slipped into one of the seats against it, remembering Rosie's words. Keep your back to the wall. Face the entrances and exits. Always be on alert.

I hadn't told my mom that Connor was on the island. I knew it would do nothing but scare her, so I had to act like everything was normal.

"Hey, Charlie?" Zoe asked as a server arrived and handed us menus. I took one with a smile. "Earth to Charlie. You look like the Terminator right now. I know you're worried about Connor, but your mom is going to know something's up if you don't stop it."

I forced myself to relax and let out a strangled laugh. "Right. Sorry."

Zoe's expression turned sympathetic. "We can always cancel, you know. Wait until all this is over. You could tell your mom you're sick, or something. You're going through a lot."

I shook my head firmly. "No. No, I'm not going to do that."

"You don't want him having that kind of control over you," Henry said, opening the drinks menu.

"That's exactly it. I've let the Ham brothers impact enough of my life. They tried to kill me. They almost killed me, multiple times in the past few days. I'm not going to hide from them, and I want them to know it."

"What are you going to do if he shows up?" Zoe asked, sounding worried.

"I have mace I got from Rosie. And a knife. She insists it's legal."

"Not a gun person, huh?" Henry asked.

"Nope. I tried it. Not really for me. And I'm sure Zoe has filled you in on the fact that I'm the last person on the planet who's allowed a Taser."

Henry chuckled. "She sure has. Anyone else and I'd be sure she was making it up. But with you, I believe it."

"I'm choosing to take that as a compliment," I said as I opened the menu.

"It's meant to be one."

"Thanks for coming with Zoe."

Henry winked at me. "I will never turn down the promise of a free meal. Besides, moms love me."

"I can imagine."

"Potential new stepdads too."

I froze. "Stepdad?"

Henry turned to Zoe, his eyes widening. "Uh-oh. I think I put my foot in it already."

"They're not there yet. But it's obviously getting serious if Carmen is inviting Lucas to meet you," Zoe said to me.

"I hadn't thought of that," I admitted. "But

you're right. It's so obvious. Okay. I'm not going to freak out."

"No, you're not," Zoe said pointedly. "You're going to have a normal dinner, where you're going to talk about normal things, and you're not going to be weird. Got it?"

"Got it," I said. I giggled slightly. "I'm sorry that this is the kind of pep talk you have to give me."

"I have to say this about being your best friend: it's never boring."

I glanced up to offer her a grateful smile. Just then, out of the corner of my eye, I spotted my mom, with Lucas next to her. "They're here."

"You can do this, Charlie," Zoe said. "It's just dinner. It's not disarming a nuclear bomb."

Somehow, I had a feeling the latter would be easier.

Chapter 22

MOM WORE A GORGEOUS LONG DRESS THAT I recognized as made by Nake'u Awai, her favorite designer. The white butterfly print on a deep purple background made her look radiant, and she carried a small white clutch at her side.

Next to her was Lucas. Standing a few inches taller than Mom, he was dressed in navy blue slacks and a white polo shirt. His hair was styled nicely, and he held my mom's hand as the two of them walked toward us. I waved, swallowing hard. It was weird, actually seeing my mom here with Lucas. Actually meeting him, instead of just staring at them from my car, wondering what was going on.

"Hello, everyone," Mom greeted us as she reached the table. "Everyone, this is Lucas. Lucas, my daughter, Charlie, her best friend, Zoe, and Zoe's boyfriend, Henry."

"Hi," Lucas said, reaching for my hand first. His grip was firm but friendly, and he looked me in the eyes while we shook. "It's nice to finally meet you. Carmen has told me so much about you."

"Not too much, I hope," I said with a nervous chuckle.

Lucas smiled good-naturedly and turned to the others.

"Henry, Zoe, it's so nice to see you both again," Mom said as she and Lucas settled in.

The waiter arrived, brought more menus, and passed them around the table before leaving again.

"You too, Carmen," Henry replied.

"And you're with Zoe. Which is great. I always thought she needed to find someone, but it's so hard with that doctor's schedule."

"Yes, what is a woman without a man at her side?" I asked dryly, and Zoe's mouth curled up into a smile behind that menu. She was all too aware of my mom's propensity to declare a young woman missing something if she happened to be single.

"And where's Jake?" Carmen asked, looking around.

"He got shot in the ass," I replied calmly.

Mom's eyes widened, and Henry had to bury

his face into the menu to hide the snort that escaped him.

"Shot? Oh my goodness! Is he all right? Can he still have children?"

I shot Mom an unimpressed look. "For someone who has literally given birth to me, you don't seem to have a great grasp on the human reproductive system. He got shot in the butt, not the balls."

"Oh, Charlie. Is he okay? Also, this isn't really a conversation to have at dinner."

I looked over at Lucas, expecting him to be looking on at us with horror. But instead, he simply looked amused with Carmen, his eyes twinkling.

"He's fine. He's at home now, resting."

"Are you sure you shouldn't be there with him? You know, creature comforts and all. You have to look after him, so he can look after you, and you can both look after my future grandchildren."

"He's a big boy. He can handle himself."

"I bet he is," Mom said, shooting me a suggestive wink.

I groaned and plucked the drinks menu from Henry's hands. "Sorry, I need this more than you do right now."

While I scanned the menu, mostly trying to figure out what beverages had the most alcohol in them so I could drink myself into oblivion and forget that Mom just had that conversation with me in front of a stranger, Lucas turned to Zoe.

"Carmen tells me you're a doctor at the hospital," he said.

She smiled. "I am. It's busy work but very rewarding. I love it."

"And you run a start-up? Between the two of you, you must be very busy," he said to Henry.

"It's true. The most complicated part of our relationship is making sure we get to see each other more than once a week. But luckily, because I own my company, it's a little bit easier for me to schedule time away. Besides, I always tell my employees that they should prioritize their lives first and foremost and that we can work the job around those. What kind of boss would I be if I didn't apply those same ideals to myself? So sometimes I let everyone know I won't be in the office until a bit later, which means I get to spend time with Zoe between shifts. Even if that's ten o'clock in the morning on a Wednesday. I'm lucky that I get to do it, because Zoe is worth it."

He looked over at her and smiled, with Zoe returning his gaze.

"I found a good one," she said. "I was always worried about what my schedule would do for my personal life. But Henry gets it."

"And he's not intimidated that Zoe totally knows like a million and one ways to murder someone without it being noticed by a doctor," I added.

This time, it was my mom's turn to groan.

"That's also true, though to be fair, I'm sure there are very few doctors out there for whom that's their first thought," Henry said.

"It would be mine, if I was a doctor."

Henry chuckled. "Is that why you aren't one?"

"One of many reasons," I admitted.

"It's no wonder your mind automatically goes to those places, though," Lucas said to me. "You're a private investigator, am I right? I've heard of you. A few friends of mine have used your services in the past. You've got a good reputation on the island."

I had to admit, Lucas was working hard to make me feel welcome, and his kind words worked. The back of my neck flushed slightly. I knew I was good at my job, but it was still cool when someone I didn't know acknowledged that. "Yeah, that's right. I guess I see a bit more murder in my line of work than most people."

The server came by then, and we all placed our drink orders. While I was just after something with copious amounts of alcohol, I ended up ordering the Monkeypod version of a Mai Tai, with lilikoi puree.

When the server left, armed with our orders, Lucas turned toward me. "Are you working on anything interesting right now? That you can speak about, of course."

"I just closed a case this afternoon, actually. The murder of the captain on board that boat just off Lanai."

Surprise registered on Lucas's face. "Really? You were involved in that?"

"Matt's mother lives in the same complex as a friend of mine. She asked me to help, and I did."

"Who did it? Are you allowed to say?"

"Sure. Unlike Zoe, I'm not bound by confidentiality laws. Besides, I'm sure it's going to be all over the news as soon as they get wind of it. It was Matt's business partner. Tony Bradley."

"I always say you should never trust anyone with two first names," Lucas replied, shaking his head.

My mouth curved into a wry smile. "I guess now's not the best time to tell you Zoe's last name is Morgan, then."

A horrified look crossed Lucas's face, and he turned to my friend. "I'm so sorry, Zoe. I meant nothing by it; it was just a quip."

"Don't worry about it," Zoe replied, waving away his apology with a gentle peal of laughter. "Besides, you never know. Maybe this has been a ruse all along, and I only pretend to be the proper one out of Charlie and me. Maybe you secretly shouldn't trust me because of my two first names."

Lucas laughed, the sound a release of the relief he obviously felt at her reaction. "Well, I'll still go to the hospital if I ever need it. Fingers crossed that I don't become one of your patients anytime soon."

"She's a great doctor. She's saved my life multiple times."

"I believe it. But go back a second. Tony Bradley. Is he the same person as Anthony Bradley?"

"Yeah, that's his legal name."

Lucas frowned. "I think I know him."

My eyebrows rose. "Oh?"

"He came in for a consultation once. I can't speak of the specifics, obviously. Attorney-client privilege. But I can say we chose not to continue a professional relationship."

"Is that lawyer talk for 'you fired him'?" I asked, a small smile creeping upward.

Lucas responded with a wink. "Can't say either way."

"You dodged a professional bullet, at the very least. And maybe a literal one too. Tony was a scammer, through and through. That's what he and Matt were doing together. It was all going to come down on him, so Tony figured he'd kill Matt and try to frame one of their victims for it. He did it on the boat so that it would look like he couldn't possibly have done it. But I got there, and now he's going to jail."

"Good for you," Lucas said with an approving nod. "It's important that people like that get put away. I wouldn't want to live on an island with someone like that walking around freely."

"Personally, I don't like Charlie working in such a business," Mom said, pursing her lips slightly. "It's dangerous work. It's unbecoming. And besides, it's practically doing the same job as Jake. How does he handle the fact that you're doing a very similar job to him?"

"Like an adult, because he's a good guy, and I wouldn't be with anyone who couldn't handle it," I replied. "We've been over this, Mom. Women can be more than secretaries and teachers these days. Not that there's anything wrong with either profession. But I can be a private investigator, and I'm good at it. Even Lucas has said it."

"It's what I've heard from coworkers."

Mom sighed. "I just want you to stay safe. And Jake too. Is he really all right? It's no small thing, being shot."

"He's going to be fine. Don't worry," I said. "Ask Zoe."

Mom turned to my best friend, who nodded.

"Yes," Zoe said. "I looked in on him at the hospital. He did have to leave early for... a work-related emergency… but he came back, and he was discharged by the doctors."

Zoe and I exchanged a quick glance. Mom didn't know that the Ham brothers had come to the island. There was no way in hell I was about to tell her either. If she freaked out that I was a private investigator, most of whose cases involved nothing more than spying on people and catching them in the middle of compromising situations, she wasn't going to handle the news that a bunch of gangsters from Seattle had come to the island to kill me well.

"It won't affect his ability to work in the future?"

"It shouldn't, Mom. It's a bullet to the butt, not the forehead."

Of course, the server chose that moment to arrive with our drinks, and she gasped slightly as she approached, unable to hide that she'd overheard.

"Don't worry," I said to her with a kind smile. "It's my boyfriend, and he'll live."

"I'm, umm, glad to hear it. Sorry," the server said quickly, placing the drinks down on the table. "Are you all ready to order?"

When the server left a minute later, Mom turned to Lucas. "I need to make Jake a care package when I get home."

"Okay, for one thing, you're not delivering it to

him directly. I am, and I'm looking through it before I give it to him," I warned. "And I swear, if you fill it with condoms and lube, he won't get it. Be normal, Mom, for once in your life. Get him some beer. Chocolate-covered macadamia nuts. He loves those. That's a care package, because I swear I'm going to force him to take some time off. Nothing else. Got it?"

Mom tutted slightly. "Do you think I don't know how to make a good care package?"

I narrowed my eyes at her. "For my boyfriend? No, definitely not. Nothing going in there needs to come from Toys 'N Us, got it?" I asked, referencing the sex shop in the middle of Kihei.

"All right, all right," Mom said, holding up her hands. "But I'm still going to include something a little bit more exciting than chocolate-covered macadamia nuts."

"Again, I'm going through it before you give it to him."

"You have the perfect opportunity with him laid up to give him what he wants," Mom said.

"And you have the opportunity now to give me what I want and stop talking about this, especially in front of other people, but obviously neither Jake nor I is getting what we want."

"You're so dramatic, Charlie. Men enjoy sex. Just look at Lucas and me."

"Nope," I replied, quickly covering my ears.

Zoe looked at the table, and the tops of Lucas's ears reddened.

"This conversation ends now, or I'm going to spill my drink all over myself and cause a scene," I said.

I knew my mom wouldn't want to cause a scene here in the nice restaurant.

"Okay, I get it," Mom finally said. "Still, the poor man. It won't affect his job?"

"No, it shouldn't. He's already been back to work. He and Liam are working another murder. Some kids found a body at a construction site."

"Oh, no," Lucas said. "I just heard about that. Do they know who the victim is?"

"I'm not sure," I lied. "But that's what Jake's been up to the past few days. He's at home now, though. Resting."

"He needs it," Zoe said. "I know he thinks this job is important, and it is, but his health is even more so."

"I know. And I think he finally gets it too. He was tired and running a bit of a fever. I told him to call me if it gets worse and that I'd take him back to the hospital. But I left him with Miss Butters watching over him, and I think he'll be okay."

"I'm glad to hear it," Lucas said.

"How about you?" I asked, turning to him. "You work in contract law. Have you always lived on the island?"

Lucas shook his head. "No. I grew up in the suburbs of Honolulu. My parents had a hard life. The war wasn't easy to them, what with them being Japanese and all. Growing up, we were poor, but I swore I was going to make a better life for myself. I worked hard and went to UH. I got into the law school there. I started working for a firm in Honolulu, working business contracts, primarily international relations. The job took me to Asia. I worked in Japan for a few years, which is where I met my wife. We fell in love, decided to get married, and came back to her home of Maui. I started my own firm here."

"What kind of contracts do you mainly deal with?" Henry asked.

"Business to business, for the most part. I won't lie; it was hard when we started out. I had no contacts on the island. But over the years, people have grown to trust me, and I've been lucky enough to build a solid portfolio of clients. Most of my work is in real estate. Leases and sales of commercial property. I'll do the odd residential project for a commercial client, but that's rare."

"And you've now got a large firm?" I asked.

"Yes, I have twelve attorneys working with me. And what Henry says about work-life balance really resonates. Historically, everyone in the law was expected to devote their whole lives to the field. I remember when I was younger, I used to feel shame and disappointment if I worked fewer than eighty hours a week. I spent my whole life devoted to my work, always thinking that one day, I'd be able to retire, and Yoko and I would spend every moment of every day together."

Lucas paused and took a deep breath, staring down at the table, his eyes unseeing. "Then, eight years ago, she was swimming on the beach when a surprise rip came out. Yoko was a good swimmer, but she panicked. Some local men went out to save her. They brought her back to shore, but it was too late. Yoko was gone."

"I'm very sorry," Zoe murmured.

"Thank you. It was the worst time of my life. Not only had I lost my wife, but I felt a tremendous amount of guilt. I loved Yoko, and I hadn't been there for her. At all. Through our whole marriage, she waited for a day that would never come. It took me a long time to come to terms with that."

Mom reached a hand over, took one of Lucas's in hers, and squeezed.

He looked over at her and smiled. "Carmen and I bonded over our losses. They were different, what with her husband having suffered a long illness, but ultimately grief is a similar process. It's losing someone. It's losing the future, when we should be focused on the present."

"Did you change anything, after Yoko died?" Henry asked quietly.

"Yes. I went back to work, and I initially poured myself into it. I thought if I could just get away from her death, it wouldn't hurt so much. But instead, every minute I sat at that desk, I thought about how I'd done this same thing throughout her whole life—and how, if I could go back and change anything, it would be that. What was the point of having a nice house? A nice car? I no longer had Yoko to enjoy the world with, and it wasn't until I lost her that I realized that."

I had to admit, I felt bad for Lucas. He had obviously loved his wife a lot.

He continued, "So, after some time, I realized that was the problem. I also stopped my staff from working as hard. They resisted, at first. As I said, in the law, the idea that you have to work ridiculous hours is engrained into you from the start. It's rather cultlike, actually. But I wanted them to enjoy their lives. I told them why. Nothing in life is certain. Everything can be taken from you in a single second."

"I think it shows what kind of person you are that you learned from that," someone said. It wasn't until a second later that I realized someone was me.

"Thank you. I just wish it hadn't cost Yoko her life with me for me to learn that lesson. But life continues, and when I met Carmen, I knew I wasn't going to make the same mistake twice. We go out at least twice a week, now."

"That's really sweet," Zoe said.

"We both know how precious life is," Mom said with a smile. "We want to enjoy ourselves. Take every day as it comes."

Okay, fine, the two of them looked very sweet together. I couldn't really find any fault in Lucas. He seemed like a genuine, good guy who was probably good for Mom in particular. And I was greatly happy for her.

The server arrived then with our food, and the conversation lulled as we focused on eating for a while. I couldn't stop glancing at the entrance. Lucas was right. Life could be so short. It could be taken away in just an instant. I wasn't going to let it happen to me. Not yet. Not ever.

Chapter 23

AFTER DINNER, THE FIVE OF US WALKED BACK down to the parking lot together.

"Where's your Jeep, Charlie?" Mom asked, looking around. "It's how I always know you're around."

"In the shop," I lied. "Had a problem with the transmission. I'm borrowing Rosie's SUV for a few days while it gets fixed."

"Well, I'll talk to you soon. It was nice having dinner."

"It was. It was really good to meet you, Lucas," I said.

A warm smile broke on his face. "Thank you. You too. Carmen has told me so much about you. To be honest, I wasn't sure what to expect, but you're her daughter, that's for sure."

"Comparing me to Mom just cost you one hundred brownie points."

Lucas laughed, then they said goodbye to Henry and Zoe before heading across the lot to Lucas's car.

"That wasn't so bad, was it?" Zoe asked, shooting me a pointed look.

"Well, apart from the bit where my mom basically said she was going to fill a basket of sex toys up for Jake and call it a care package."

Zoe's mouth flickered into a smile. "You started that, though. I mean, by her normal standards. She didn't make a single comment about how I was single for so long she thought I might be a lesbian."

"That's true. Because everyone knows lesbians have to hide their relationships entirely these days."

Henry chuckled. "It's fun to experience firsthand that Zoe's stories about Carmen aren't entirely made up."

"You should try being her daughter. I swear, she's not coming to my wedding, because she's going to insist on coming into the bedroom to make sure the damn thing is consummated."

"Oooh, we're talking a wedding now, are we?" Zoe asked, shooting me a wink.

"*In general*," I replied. "Jake and I have not talked marriage. Ever."

"Fair enough," Zoe replied with a giggle.

"Although I did tell him I loved him the other day," I said quietly.

Zoe immediately reached over and gave me a hug. "Oh, I'm so proud of you."

"Thanks," I muttered. "I guess the thought that I almost lost him to a random robber's bullet kind of got the better of me."

"Or—and just hear me out here—you fell in love with a man, and you told him that, like the emotionally stable and not-at-all-repressed young woman you're trying to be."

"It could be that, too," I admitted.

"That's a big moment for you, Charlie."

"What happened to the man who shot Jake?" Henry asked.

I stood in stunned silence at the question. "You know… I don't actually know. I assumed he was taken into custody. Liam was there, after all. But he might have been taking care of Jake."

I couldn't believe it. How had I not asked? With everything else that had happened—being worried initially that Jake was going to die, being kidnapped by the Ham brothers, and then trying to bring them down—I had completely and totally forgotten to find out what happened to the person who shot Jake.

"Shit," I muttered, pulling out my phone and looking for Liam's number in my contacts. He was there, along with a puke emoji. I mashed the call button and shifted my weight from foot to foot as I waited for him to answer.

"Hello?" he answered a few seconds later.

"Hey, it's Charlie. I need you to tell me something: what happened to the guy who shot Jake? Is he in custody?"

The other end of the line was silent for a few seconds. "Umm, Jake told me I wasn't allowed to talk to you about it," he finally admitted.

I bared my teeth, even though I knew Liam couldn't see it. "He told you not to tell me?"

"Yeah. When he was being rushed to the hospital. He told me not to say anything."

"Okay, look here, Liam. You can either tell me right now what happened, or I'm going to go to every single donut shop on this island and tell them you like to walk around your house with a donut hanging off your dick like the world's most disgusting inner tube. Then, I'm going to tell them you fuck the cream ones through the little hole. You'll never be able to show your face at a single store again, you got me? So I'm going to ask you again, what happened to the guy?"

"You're a fucking pervert, you know that?" Liam snapped at me. "I don't know what Jake sees in you."

"The whole island will think you're the pervert if you don't tell me what I want to know."

"You wouldn't," he growled.

"You know me. You know what I've done. Is that really a risk you're willing to take?"

Hatred flowed through the phone line between us, but eventually, Liam cracked. "Fine. Fine, I'll tell you. Yeah, the guy got away. I figured saving Jake's life was more important than catching the guy. We know who he is. We just have to find him again."

I closed my eyes and took a deep breath. "You made the right call saving Jake."

"I think so too."

"What's his name?"

"The robber?"

"Yes, obviously the robber."

"Jake will kill me if I tell you."

"What flavour donut do you think would be the weirdest to fuck? Raspberry? It looks a bit like blood, doesn't it?"

"Jesus, do you never stop? Fine. Jerod Nash. Local moron. Drug dealer. But you can't tell Jake that came from me, okay?"

"You got it. I assume he's still on your radar and you're going after him?"

"Not right now. Jake insisted. He wanted to work that case in the construction site." Liam's tone turned a little bit snarky. "So really, it's because of you that Jake's shooter hasn't been found. We would have gone after him if you hadn't brought those people from Seattle here."

"Ah yes, everyone knows the cops are the first people who should blame victims."

"And stay away from my donut shops."

I cackled as Liam hung up on me. He was a terrible cop, but at least he'd given me what I needed.

"He got away?" Henry asked when I put the phone down.

I nodded. "Yes. But not for long. As soon as this is over, I'm going after Jerod Nash and making sure he goes to jail for trying to kill Jake."

"Just jail?" Zoe asked in a warning tone.

I nodded. "Yes. Jake wouldn't want anything else to happen. He doesn't even want me going after him. He told Liam not to tell me."

"Yeah, we kind of figured that part out," Henry said with an amused smile.

"I'm going to find the guy," I said, steeling my voice, my jaw hardening.

Zoe shot me an unimpressed look. "No, you're not."

"Of course I am. He shot Jake."

"Yeah, and you know who should want him caught? Jake. And yet, Jake prioritized the California gang ahead of this guy. Do you know who he is?"

"A local scumbag, according to Liam."

"There you go. So, he's local. He's probably not going anywhere. He might even think he got away with it. You can't take everybody on all at once. You need to focus your energy on one thing."

I was practically vibrating with built-up energy. "There are just so many people out there that need to go to jail."

"I know," Zoe said. "I agree with you. But this is a classic situation where you need to focus on one at a time. Right now, Jerod Nash isn't a big threat. He's not actively trying to kill Jake. He's not actively trying to kill you. This is why Jake made Liam back off—because Jake understood the stakes. Connor Ham *is* trying to kill you. Deal with him first. And after that's finished, then you can try to find Jerod."

I sighed. "Why does everything always have to sound so reasonable when you say it?"

"Because I take a step back and think about things before immediately jumping headfirst into the next thing I think of," she replied pointedly.

I blew out a puff of air. "It's just all so much."

"Yes. And you can't do it all yourself. Not today. You need to catch Connor. Make sure he's arrested. It's what Jake wants too. He'd rather see you safe than see his shooter behind bars."

"Okay," I grumbled. "Fine. You're right. I'll

take care of Connor. Jerod is a Future Charlie problem."

"Exactly. You've got it. It's going to be okay, Charlie. You're going to get justice, for yourself and for Jake. But if you split your energy, you make it more likely that you're going to fail at both."

Zoe was right. As always. I said goodbye to her and Henry then climbed into Rosie's SUV and headed back to Dot's place. All things considered, dinner had gone well.

I was nearly sure Lucas wasn't a sociopath.

And once Connor was taken care of, I would bring Jake's shooter to justice.

"SO, HOW WAS DINNER?" ROSIE ASKED WHEN I entered. Middie rubbed herself against my leg, begging for pats.

"Great," I said, leaning down and scratching Middie behind the ears. "Well, about as well as can be expected, anyway. I like Lucas. He seems nice."

"If you need me to do a deep dive into his history, just say the word," Dot said, holding her fingers over the keyboard expectantly and wiggling them. "I'm more than happy to do so, especially for your mom."

I shook my head. "Thanks. As much as a part of my brain is screaming at me to take you up on that, I think the grown-up thing to do here is to let it go. I met him. There were no red flags. He seems like a genuinely good guy."

Rosie frowned. "So did Ted Bundy."

"All right, topic change," Dot interrupted. "I spent this afternoon studying pictures of Connor Ham, while that beast ate my plants and used my toilet."

"That's so weird," I agreed.

"I was talking about Rosie," Dot joked, cackling to herself. "Anyway, I eventually realized he has one of those fancy GPS watches. You know, the ones people use to track their exercise. I managed to figure out the brand, and I got into their back end while you were at dinner, Charlie. I had to work to narrow it down, but I think I've got him."

Rosie and I immediately made a beeline for the computer, peering over Dot's shoulder at the screen. It was a dark-mode map of Maui, with the outlines of roads and buildings in dark grey over the screen. In the center, a single dot flashed pale blue, over and over.

"He's just outside the hotel," I said, recognizing the spot on the map.

"He is," Dot confirmed. "And he's on the move."

The three of us watched soundlessly as the little blue dot began to move toward the hotel parking lot. It stopped for a minute then moved again, faster this time.

"He's gotten his hands on another vehicle," I said.

"Must have used another identity. He's burning them up like old love letters," Dot agreed.

"The question is, where is he heading?" Rosie murmured.

About three or four minutes later, we had our answer. The dot had gone up the highway and turned off at the exit that led to the building where I lived.

"Shit," I muttered, pulling out my phone and immediately dialing Zoe's number. As soon as she answered, I practically shouted into the phone, "Are you home? Don't answer the door. Connor Ham is coming to our building. And so am I. This ends now."

Chapter 24

LUCKILY, ABOUT THIRTY SECONDS LATER, THE DOT stopped. Connor Ham drove slowly past my building, but he kept going past it then stopped the car along the road farther down the street. He didn't get out.

"He's looking for Queenie, I bet," I said. "That's why he drove past. He's waiting for me to get there."

"This is it," Rosie said. "I have a plan."

Ten minutes later, with everything between us decided, I was back in Queenie. I patted the dashboard of my old Jeep as I stepped in. "I missed you, girl. Now, let's go get this guy."

I drove home, my heart jackhammering in my chest. I was all too aware that waiting for me was a man who was not only going to try to kill me but try to make me hurt while doing it. After all, I was responsible for both his brothers' deaths.

He wasn't going to let me off easy for that, even if it was their own faults.

I couldn't let him know I was onto him. We specifically decided I should drive past his car when I headed home so that he would know I was on my way. I was bait, and while ideally, this would end with the big fish being reeled in, that didn't make the situation any less stressful for the worm on the hook.

Pulling into the space, I checked the rearview mirror then locked the car and exited. It took everything in my power not to look toward the street. Dot told me she would text me straightaway if Connor was on the move, so I tried not to panic.

I would know when he was coming. He wasn't going to shoot me from afar. It was all going to be fine.

Walking to the front door, I stepped into the building and climbed up the stairs. My phone pinged in my pocket, and I closed my eyes for a second before reading Dot's text.

He's on his way.

I expected I would have about twenty, maybe thirty seconds of a head start on Connor. After all, that was how long had passed between when I walked in the door and when I received Dot's text.

I was halfway down the hallway, rifling

through my purse for my keys, when I was suddenly hit from behind.

I yelped and dropped my bag, the contents spilling out onto the hallway. Immediately, I acted. I used the momentum to continue moving forward, running down the hall, Connor's footsteps not far behind.

He reached me before I got to the stairwell door. Connor grabbed me by the hair, whipped me around, and threw me against the wall.

Pain coursed through me as I fell to the floor, but before I could take a single breath, he was on me. He kicked me, knocking the wind out of me as his shoe connected with my middle.

I gasped for air, desperate right now for nothing but to survive.

"You killed my brothers," Connor snarled at me.

"They brought it on themselves," I wheezed in reply.

"Tell me how Brandon died, and I'll make your death quick. The one mercy I can offer you."

I grinned. "Your brother tried to kill me. But nature got to him first. The blowhole, up north. It was dark, and I lured him toward it. And the other one. They both went for it, and your brother got hit by the water. He tried to escape. He fell off the rocks and toward the water. I could have saved him, you know. But I stood there, and I watched him get weaker. And then, he couldn't hold on anymore. And you know what he did? He cried. Like a big, dumb baby. He wanted his mommy. He didn't want to die. And I was laughing as he let go."

Okay, I was embellishing for dramatic effect. Just a little bit. What could I say? I was a dramatic person.

But I figured no matter what happened, I wanted Connor to know that his brother was a coward who spent his last few moments suffering. Besides, it wasn't that far from the truth.

"You liar," Connor snarled, and he kicked at me again, but this time, I was ready.

I grabbed at his leg as he kicked me, clutching it against me. I winced as pain coursed through me once more, but I didn't let go. I yanked, knocking Connor off balance.

"Fucking bitch," he cried as he fell to the floor, landing with a loud thud that was barely cushioned by the thin carpet.

"This bitch already killed two of you, and I'm happy to go three for three," I growled as I jumped up and launched myself directly onto Connor.

He wasn't expecting me to jump on top of him, and he held up his hands to stop me, right as I launched a knee directly into his crotch.

Connor let out a loud groan as he rolled over away from me and curled into the fetal position.

I was about to strike again when he suddenly reached out and hit wildly with his fist, connecting with the side of my cheek.

The pain that seared through my face stopped me momentarily, long enough for him to throw me off and onto the floor. I rolled and hit the far wall, my head hitting the baseboard.

My vision started going dark, and stars flew in front of me, but there was no way I was giving up now.

"You're going to die here tonight," Connor snarled as he slowly got to his feet.

I tried to do the same, but my balance was off.

Connor kicked at me, aiming for my face, but I had just enough sense left that I whipped my head to the side at the last second, causing him to miss me and embed his foot into the drywall.

I scrambled to my feet while he struggled to release himself from the wall's grip, which gave me just enough time to shove him as hard as I could.

Connor's leg was still stuck in the wall, and as he fell, I heard a crack, and he cried out in pain.

"My knee! My fucking knee." Connor grabbed at his leg and yanked it free then struggled to his feet just as I launched myself at him once more.

He sidestepped me and threw me down the hall, and I stumbled, falling to the ground. My hands burned as they slid along the carpet, the stitches pulling against my skin for additional torture, but as I got up, my heart dropped.

Connor had just pulled a gun out from his waistband and levelled it directly at me.

"You know, I wasn't going to use this," he snarled. "I wanted you to hurt. I wanted you to suffer. But you're not going to go down easy. You're like a rabid dog."

"Thank you."

"That wasn't a compliment," Connor practically shouted, the gun trembling in his hand. "Why are you so fucking crazy? I'm going to kill you. I'm going to put you down. You belong in the ground."

He was fifteen feet away from me and had a clear shot. There was nowhere for me to go. In short, I was screwed.

And then, at that precise moment, the door to the stairwell behind us opened, and my neighbour Franny walked through, followed closely by her father, Frank.

"Holy shit, Franny, get down," I shouted as Connor turned to see what was going on.

I no longer cared what happened to me. All that mattered was that Franny came out of this okay.

"Do what you want to me," I said quickly to

Connor. "But leave them alone. They're innocent."

If she noticed the gun, Franny made no indication of it. Frank was frozen in place against the wall, flattened against it as if he might be able to disappear into it.

"Get out of here," Connor shouted at them, motioning with the gun for them to head back to the stairs.

"Franny, come here, right now," Frank ordered, reaching for his daughter. But she had gotten to the contents of my purse, splayed out across the floor toward her.

"Is this man trying to hurt you, Charlie?" Franny asked, bearing the picture-perfect look of an innocent little girl.

"Me?" Connor asked, keeping the gun trained on me but occasionally glancing toward Frank, just to be sure he wasn't about to try anything.

He really didn't have much to worry about; Frank looked as though every ounce of blood had completely escaped his face and settled somewhere else in his body.

"You don't have to worry," Connor said, his voice coated in sweet honey. "I'm not doing anything to Charlie that she doesn't deserve."

"Good," Franny said, looking up at him, something in her hand. "Because Charlie's my friend. And she doesn't deserve to be hurt."

Franny's voice was falsely high. She must have been terrified, poor kid. She came off as the sweetest little girl, and the one thing I was grateful for was that as much as Connor seemed to have no qualms putting a bullet in the middle of my forehead, he was going to let Franny get away.

"I'm sure you think that. But Charlie killed some people. People I love."

That was when I realized Franny had been sitting among the items that had spilled out from my purse. And her little fingers were wrapped around the canister of Mace Rosie had given me.

"They probably deserved it," Franny said, just as she pointed the canister directly at Connor's face and blasted him with the mace.

Connor screamed. He clutched at his face, and the gun went off, the bullet shooting harmlessly into the ceiling.

"Franny, run, now," I ordered.

She did as I said, grabbing her father's hand on the way out as the two of them escaped back down the stairs the way they came.

My eight-year-old neighbour had just saved my life.

Connor was clutching at his eyes, still screaming, the gun still in his hand. I hesitated for a second. I could always try to get it off him. But that was a risky move right now; he could point it and shoot it at me, or shoot me accidentally.

On the other hand, waiting for him to get his eyesight back so he could shoot me with good aim also didn't feel like a winning plan right now.

I ran forward and tackled him. The gun clattered to the floor while Connor let out a shout of surprise. Or pain. I wasn't entirely sure which, but I was pretty happy with either possibility.

And then Vesper's door opened, down the hall.

"What's going on out here?" she shouted, coming down, armed with something.

Not until she was a few feet away did I realize what was in her hand. It was Dildo Daggins, her giant vibrator, which she was holding by the tip and waving around her head like the world's most perverted lasso.

"You leave Charlie alone," she shouted as she threw herself into the fray, her prosthetic leg not holding her back from getting involved.

As Connor fought back against me, he grabbed the gun from the ground. The two of us grappling for control, Vesper began hitting him over the head with the dildo, repeatedly bashing the thick end against his even thicker skull.

The gun went off again, and I braced for pain but felt nothing.

Vesper was still going strong. I didn't know where the bullet had gone, but it looked like neither one of us was hit. For now.

"I'm going to kill all of you," Connor screamed.

"Dildo Daggins has defeated better men than you," Vesper yelled back, and she swung it one last time against the side of Connor's head.

His eyes rolled up into the back of his head, and he fell backward, stumbling, the gun falling to the floor as he collapsed, unconscious.

It took a second for me to register what had happened.

As soon as I saw Connor on the floor, my gaze fell to the gun. Vesper picked it up. She looked down at it then pointed it at Connor. "What do you think? Textbook self-defense case if I pull the trigger?"

"Don't," I said, shaking my head. "You don't want that kind of legal action on your back. Besides, Connor deserves to go to jail."

"You're supposed to be fun, you know," Vesper complained.

"Sorry I won't let you murder an unconscious guy, even if he does deserve it."

"You should."

"Thanks for the help."

"Dildo Daggins comes in handy for more things than you know," Vesper said with a wink.

Suddenly, the door to my apartment creaked open, and Zoe poked her head out. "Is it safe to come out? Does anyone need medical attention? I've already called 9-1-1."

"We're fine," I said, and Zoe breathed a visible sigh of relief as she emerged from the apartment, first aid kit in hand. "Thank God."

"Go find Franny and Frank," I ordered. "They came up early, and they'll have had a shock. At least, Frank did."

"He shot me," Vesper announced, and I gaped at her.

Chapter 25

"WHAT?"

Vesper hoisted up her leg to reveal the thigh of her prosthetic. Sure enough, a dime-sized hole was poking right through the plastic. Vesper pulled off the limb, dug around in the hole area, and pulled out a bullet. "Luckily I'd already lost this leg."

I thought I was going to pass out from relief.

"You are lucky; if that had hit your femoral, you might have bled out," Zoe said. "I'm going to find Franny and Frank. Everything here is okay?"

"Sure is," I said as I reached Jake's door and began pounding on it. "Hey, you! Wake up!"

No answer came, so I dug through my pile of things on the floor until I pulled out the spare key for Jake's apartment.

"Oooh," Vesper teased when she saw where I

was headed. "We're exchanging keys now, huh? Things must be getting serious with you two."

"Oh, not right now," I muttered. "Watch this guy, will you?"

"You got it. He wakes up, I'm shooting him."

"Okay, deal," I agreed as I unlatched the door and entered. Jake was in bed, completely passed out. I placed a hand on his forehead; he was running a high fever.

"Shit," I muttered. I supposed it wasn't fully necessary for him to be here. Zoe had called the police. They would be here soon. And Jake obviously needed to go back to the hospital if he had slept through what just happened.

But as I was turning to go, he came to.

"Charlie?" he murmured sleepily. "What's going on?"

"Connor Ham is unconscious outside. He's ready to get taken to jail."

"I'll bring him in," Jake said, and he started getting out of bed.

"No," I ordered, pressing a hand to his chest. "You need to go to the hospital. I mean it. I'm calling an ambulance for you now. Stay here."

Jake shook his head and got up with a groan. "No. At least let me cuff him."

"Fine," I agreed. Jake got out of bed and grabbed his gun and badge from the side table, along with his handcuffs. I followed him as he headed out into the hallway.

Vesper had the gun pointed at Connor, and she was kicking at him gently with her toe.

"Come on. Wake up, so I can shoot you. I promise to hit something nonfatal. Maybe a knee, or something. After all, you shot me in the leg."

"Vesper," Jake said, and my neighbour jumped about a foot.

"Why don't we pretend you didn't hear any of that, huh?" she asked with a grin. Then, she got a good look at him. "Damn. Are you okay?"

"Okay enough to cuff this asshole," Jake replied, rolling Connor over unceremoniously and putting the handcuffs on him.

"Zoe?" I called out down the stairs. "Can you come here? I think Jake needs you."

Connor was still unconscious when Zoe returned. She took one look at Jake and ordered him to sit down on the floor.

"You're running a high fever. I'm calling an ambulance," she said immediately, pulling out her phone. "You're going back to the hospital now."

"I need to arrest Connor," Jake muttered.

"You did that," Zoe told him, her tone firm but kind. "He's under arrest. He can't do anything. The other police will be here soon, and they'll take him into custody. But you need the hospital."

I crouched next to the two of them, hovering

over Jake and feeling helpless. "What's happening?"

"He has an infection. It might have been caused by the surgery. It might be from having exerted himself too much afterward. But he needs to get back to the hospital straightaway, where they'll take care of him."

My heart lurched upward into my throat. "He's going to be okay, though, right?"

Zoe looked over and took one of my hands in hers. "Almost certainly yes, Charlie. This is a bad situation, but it's not life-threatening yet. He's going to be fine."

"I should have insisted on him coming to dinner," I muttered. "You would have noticed right away that something was wrong."

"It's okay, Charlie. It was the right call for him not to come. And we got to him. We're here. He's here. And he's going to be fine."

In the background, I began to hear sirens. The police were on their way. And so was an ambulance. It was going to be okay. Jake was going to be okay.

And Connor Ham was under arrest. He was out of my life completely.

Frank and Franny emerged from the stairwell just then.

"Franny," I said to her gratefully, opening my

arms, which the little girl ran right into. "Thank you. You were a superspy today."

She pulled away and beamed at me, smiling from ear to ear. "That was the coolest thing I have ever done."

"That was the most terrifying thing you've ever done," Frank corrected. "When we get home, we're going to have a very long conversation about safety around guns. Just because you like to read about spies doesn't mean you are one."

"But Dad, it worked! I stopped the bad guy," Franny complained. "And I didn't get hurt."

"This time," Frank said firmly. "You're very lucky you weren't hurt. That man had a *gun*, Franny. A real gun. Don't they teach you what to do if someone is shooting when you're at school?"

Franny rolled her eyes. "Of course we do school shooter drills, Dad. But I've read a lot of books. And besides, he wasn't shooting. I'm okay."

"Your dad is right," I pointed out. "I'm very glad you're okay, Franny, but that was very dangerous."

"We're going inside and talking about this. Where did you even learn to use Mace?"

"The internet."

Frank opened the door to her apartment and held it wide, waiting for his daughter to enter. Franny's face fell, and she trudged over the threshold and into the apartment. He shot me a dirty look before they went inside. Evidently, he held me partially responsible for what had happened.

I couldn't exactly blame him there.

A few seconds later, the police arrived up the stairs, guns at the ready.

"He's under arrest," I said, motioning to Connor. "Detective Jake Llewelyn cuffed him and is now being treated by Doctor Morgan. Please, take him away and Mirandize him properly."

The two officers on the scene glanced around in confusion. One was about my age, and one was even younger. Both looked like they'd struggled their whole lives to grow beards. Or carry dumbbells heavier than twenty pounds.

"I need to take a statement," one of them stammered.

"I'll deal with all of that," Jake said, pulling his badge from his waistband with obvious difficulty and holding it up to the officers. "Book this man for murder. And attempted murder. I'll take care of the rest."

The order from their superior officer spurred both men into action.

One of them hoisted Connor to his feet; he was just starting to stir, and he groaned as he was lifted. "What happened?" He muttered.

"Sir, you're under arrest for murder and

attempted murder," one of the officers began to recant. "You have the right to remain silent. Anything you say can and will be used against you in a court of law."

As Connor regained full consciousness and everything came flooding back to him, he looked over at me. "You!" he shouted. "You did this! This is all your fault. You're not going to get away with this."

Connor began to struggle against the officers, trying to get to me to attack me.

I stood to the side, grinned, and gave him a finger wave. "Enjoy prison, Connor. It's been a long time coming for you."

Connor gave a Herculean effort to break free from the grasp of the police officers, but it was no use. They had a firm grip on him.

"I'll come escort you to jail," I sang, following the police as they led Connor toward the stairs.

"I'm coming too," Jake announced, rising slowly to his feet.

Zoe looked concerned but didn't stop him. "I'll come too. The ambulance will be here soon. I can get the EMTs up to speed on your situation."

As they walked down the stairs, following the officers, Connor continued to scream and shout. Apparently, he was not going to take advantage of his right to remain silent.

"This is fucking bullshit! It's bullshit! I'm innocent. This is all her fault. She did this to me! And that stupid little kid. Arrest the kid. She deserves to go to jail."

As we walked down the stairs, a wave of relief hit me. It really was all over.

Outside, red and blue lights illuminated the side of the building, like a law enforcement-themed rave. The two officers were leading Connor toward a waiting police vehicle.

The three of us were behind him.

"Let's wait here," I said quietly, stopping the others.

"Why?" Jake asked, pausing and frowning. "What's going on?"

A split second later, Connor collapsed.

I walked over to him. He was staring at the sky, lifeless.

In the middle of his forehead was a small red dot. And then all hell broke loose.

Chapter 26

"CHARLIE, GET DOWN," JAKE ORDERED, GRABBING both Zoe and me around the waist and shoving us back to the entrance of the building.

"Jake, hold on," I said. "It's okay."

He immediately shifted into cop mode, his gun pulled out and levelled as his eyes scanned the outside, methodically searching for the person who had just killed Connor Ham.

"The enemy of your enemy is not necessarily your friend," Jake muttered, on the alert.

"No, but in this case, I happen to know that she is," I said slowly.

Jake paused and looked at me carefully. "You know who killed Connor?"

I shrugged. "I might have an idea."

Jake swore under his breath. "I cannot believe you, Charlie. You just killed a man."

"Technically, no. I was right here, with you and Zoe. I had nothing to do with it."

"You know damn well what I mean."

"And I know what he was doing to me. It wasn't going to be enough for him to be behind bars. Ever. He had to die. Do you disagree?"

Jake and I stared each other down. His brow was layered with sweat. I hadn't realized how deep his eyes looked, or how his skin had taken on a slight grayish tinge.

"I do," Jake finally said. "You can't murder someone just because of what they might do to you."

"Okay, you're too sick for an argument right now," Zoe interrupted. "Now come on. I see the lights of the ambulance. We'll deal with the fallout of Connor's death later."

"You're one hundred percent sure it's safe to go out there?" Jake asked.

I nodded. "I trust the person behind that gun with my life."

"We're never going to find them, are we?" Jake asked.

"Nope."

The three of us exited the building once more. The two officers were crouched behind the police car. Connor Ham's body lay abandoned, alone in the middle of the complex parking lot.

As we walked past the corpse toward the

ambulance, I got one more look at him. His face, lit up in blues and reds, was contorted with anger. His mouth was slightly open. He had been shot mid-yell.

I hope he cursed my name as he died, because he was going to curse it all the way down to hell.

It was over. It was finally over. All three Ham brothers were dead. Their organization was destined to collapse with the head honchos gone. And I could live the rest of my life in peace.

I couldn't believe it.

"Post-surgical patient presenting with a fever and sweating, probable infection," Zoe called out, breaking me from my thoughts. She had rushed ahead as the EMTs jumped out of the ambulance. "He's a police officer; he was shot in the gluteus maximus."

"Haha, you got shot in the butt," I said to Jake, trying to joke.

"Really? Now?" He shot me a look.

"What can I say? Humour is my coping mechanism."

Before Jake had a chance to reply, someone whisked him toward the ambulance. A blood pressure machine was being wrapped around his arm.

"Come on, Charlie," Zoe said, wrapping an arm around my waist. "We can go and meet him at the hospital."

I nodded numbly. It wasn't until we turned away that I realized I wanted to be with Jake.

"Can't I go with him?"

"Let the EMTs work," she said. "I'll drive you."

I knew Zoe was right. I could have ridden along in the ambulance, but I was a wreck, and I didn't want Jake to see that. I didn't want him to notice how worried I was, despite Zoe's assurances that he was going to be fine.

What would have happened if I'd just let him sleep through the night? If Connor Ham hadn't come to kill me?

Zoe and I raced upstairs. I scooped everything from the floor back into my purse, and as I climbed into Zoe's car, I pulled out my phone and sent Rosie a text.

Nice shot.

Her reply came through a minute later. *Easy as pie.*

The corners of my mouth curled into a small smile.

Jake has some sort of infection. I think it's complication from the surgery. He's on the way to the hospital in the ambulance, and Zoe is driving me there.

Keep us up to date. We're here when you're ready.

I had the best friends ever.

"How are you doing?" Zoe asked, shooting a concerned glance my way for a split second before turning her eyes back to the road. "Did Connor hurt you?"

"Nothing that won't heal. I think. My stomach is sore."

"Normally I only hear you say that after you've eaten something stupid."

I cracked another smile. "Vesper got shot in the prosthetic leg."

"I saw. But how about *you*? You're sure you're fine, physically? Your face is cut."

"That was probably from when he punched me. I didn't realize," I admitted. "But I mean it; I'm fine. I've suffered worse."

"There are prisoners of war in ancient times who have suffered worse than you. That doesn't mean you're okay."

"I am. I promise. Would I lie to you about this?"

Zoe shot me another look. "You could have a bullet in your shoulder, and you would tell me you're fine."

"I know. But this time, I really mean it."

"Okay. Connor's dead. Who was it, Rosie?"

"Yes. The plan was for Jake to arrest Connor, and then she would shoot him. Things went a little bit off the rails, though."

"No kidding," Zoe said dryly.

"He wasn't supposed to get a jump on me. I also didn't realize Jake was on the brink of death. I was going to come into the apartment and tell you to lock yourself in the bedroom with Coco, and then when he came in, I was going to stab him. Somewhere nonlethal. Maybe the stomach."

Zoe's eyebrows rose. "You truly have no understanding of anatomy if you think a stomach wound can't be fatal."

"I was only going to stab him a little bit," I argued.

"I can't believe that's a sentence that just came out of your mouth."

"Anyway, he surprised me in the hall. Luckily, Franny and Vesper came to my aid. I never thought I'd have to thank Vesper's dildo for saving my life. Or that I'd see a man bludgeoned half to death with one."

Zoe laughed. "There's a first time for everything. I've actually seen that once."

"No way. I thought all you saw in the ER was weird things stuck up butts."

"That's a big one. But when I was doing my residency, years ago, a guy walked in on his girlfriend, in the middle of her using the dildo on herself. Anyway, it turned into a big argument about how he couldn't pleasure her."

"Oops."

"Exactly. It ended with her slapping him across the face with it, and it broke his cheekbone."

My mouth dropped open. "No way."

"Yes way. He came into the ER, but he wasn't worried about the broken bone."

"No?"

"He was more worried about the shape of the bruise that had formed on his cheek."

I snorted. "Oh man. Yeah, I bet."

"He wanted to know what he could do to hide the bruise. I had to give him the unfortunate news that bruises aren't the kind of thing we could just make go away, and he was going to have to wait for it to fade away on its own."

"I bet he loved that."

"He wasn't pleased," Zoe confirmed. "But he had no choice other than to live with it. There are best practices, but there's no magic bruise remover."

"Don't I know it. My stomach will probably need it. I think he ruptured my spleen."

"I'll get you checked in when we arrive."

"I don't mean it. I don't think my spleen is burst."

"Do you know what a ruptured spleen feels like?"

"No," I admitted.

"You know who does know? Your best friend."

"You're just looking for an excuse to feel me up."

"Always. Everyone knows the spleen is the sexiest part of the body."

"You're a doctor. You're not supposed to have favourite body parts."

"I didn't say it was my favorite. I said it was the sexiest."

"Besides, how did a conversation about a dildo-shaped bruise turn into sexy spleen chat?"

"Normally I would blame you, but I think this one is actually on me. My bad."

"You're trying to stop me from thinking about Connor, aren't you?"

"Him being shot was a surprise. But apparently, it wasn't to you."

I shrugged. "What can I say? It's been obvious for a little while now that it was him or me. It wasn't going to be enough to put him in jail. It was going to be a tough case to prove. We all knew it. He's slippery. He's slithered out of the fingers of the law before, and if he did it again, what then? I couldn't take that risk."

"He's actively tried to kill you multiple times. At this point, if you ask me, it's self-defense. Even if the bullet came from a sniper rifle on a nearby rooftop. Speaking of, remind me every single day to never get on Rosie's bad side, okay?"

I laughed. "Yeah, that's priority number one for me too. She is terrifying. In the best way."

"She did not miss."

"She never does."

"Where was she?"

"I'm not sure. She said for everyone's sake she wasn't going to tell us. I knew she was waiting outside, but that's all I knew."

"That's why you insisted on coming along. You wanted to see it happen." Zoe glanced my way once more.

"I did," I admitted. "But not in a gross way."

"I'd love to learn what other non-gross ways there are to want to watch someone get shot."

"I needed the finality of it. I needed to see it happen. Or at least see his body. And I figured if I wasn't right there, they wouldn't let me come out to see it."

"Gee, I wonder why."

"I mean it, though. I had to see it. I had to be sure. They terrorized me, Zoe. For years. Ever since I found that finger."

"I know," she said quietly.

"I moved back in with my mom, for goodness's sake."

Zoe giggled. "Truly the worst thing to ever happen to you."

"At the very least, I had a lot of uncomfortable conversations. And then there was the last few months. Knowing they were coming. Not knowing how to handle it. Being chased out on the Acid War Zone Trail. It's been a lot, Zoe. And I just want it to stop."

"You have. It's over now," Zoe said. "You can focus on you. And Jake."

"You're not lying to me, right? He is going to be okay?"

"Yes. At least, he should be. With the human body, you never really can know for sure, but while it looks bad, we caught it early. They're going to sort him out."

"Could it be because the surgeons left the bullet in his ass?"

"It's possible but unlikely. I think it's probably because he decided to go right back to work despite the doctors telling him explicitly not to do that. Especially after what happened when he saved you in that garage."

"He just wanted Connor Ham caught," I said quietly. "He even prioritized it over finding the person who shot *him*."

"You know Jake. Are you especially surprised by this?" Zoe asked dryly.

"No. He loves me, Zoe. He said he loves me."

"I know. No man does the things Jake does for a woman he doesn't love."

"I love him too," I said quietly.

"I know. It's going to be okay, Charlie. He's going to be okay."

This wasn't the first time this week she'd told me that.

ZOE TURNED OUT TO BE RIGHT, AS ALWAYS. JAKE was okay. The ambulance beat us to the hospital, and by the time Zoe and I arrived, he'd been admitted. Zoe insisted that she do a physical exam before I was allowed to go see him, and fifteen minutes later, with blood samples taken to be safe and a physical exam that showed no sign of a burst spleen, I was walking to where they were keeping Jake. I pulled the curtain aside to find him lying in bed, an IV drip attached to his arm.

As soon as I walked in, he looked serious. "You had that planned, didn't you? Who shot him? Was it Dot? Or Rosie? She puts on a good innocent old lady show, but she's more than she seems, isn't she?"

"I don't think you want to know the answer to any of those questions, do you?"

Jake sighed. "No, I don't."

"You understand why I did it."

I grabbed a chair from the corner of the room and dragged it over next to the bed. Then, I sat down on it, reaching across and taking Jake's hand.

Jake's voice was barely audible when he replied, "I do."

"You're an officer of the law. And I get that. But you, more than anyone, know that sometimes the law can't protect people. Your job is to get there after the fact. After a crime has already been committed. And Connor Ham wasn't going to commit any crime against me other than murder. He had to be stopped."

"He'd been arrested," Jake protested, but his argument was weak; we both knew he didn't really believe it.

"We both know he would have hired the best lawyer on the island. Gotten them to do everything they could to get him off. Well, okay, second-best lawyer. The best is Zoe's mom, and she never would have represented him."

Jake managed a small smile. "You're not wrong."

"So there were no other options. Don't worry —the police will never solve this case. It'll go cold. It will be written off as a rival gang coming over and killing the Ham brothers while they were away on holiday. Believe me, it'll never come back to whoever fired that shot."

"There's so much about your life I still don't know about," Jake said, shaking his head incredulously.

"It's okay. You know about the most important bits."

"I do get it, though. And I'm not mad. I'm not even upset. I was, initially. But I think more than anything, I'm relieved. Relieved that I don't have to worry about you anymore. That I don't have to keep my head on a swivel. That I don't have to think about the Ham brothers anymore."

"Me too. But listen, you were also keeping something from me."

"Oh?"

"Jerod."

Jake closed his eyes and leaned back in the hospital bed. "How did you find out?"

"I threatened to tell every donut shop on the island that Liam walks around with them on his dick like a cock ring if he didn't give me a name."

Jake groaned. "The worst part is, I'm sure you're telling the truth."

"He shot you. He needs to be brought to justice."

"And he will be. Now that Connor Ham is no longer a threat, we can focus on him. But I didn't want you distracted before. Jerod isn't going anywhere. He's a local moron."

"A moron who shot you," I pointed out. "I want his head."

"How very French Revolutionary of you. He'll be arrested. Don't worry. We found him once. We're going to find him again."

"The 'we' in that sentence had better not mean you." My voice got quieter. "You almost died. Again. And this all because you tried to save me. Over and over. It's time for you to rest.

Let me find Jerod. I'll make sure he sees justice. And I even have someone who can put a bullet in his brain for you, if that's the route you want to go."

Jake snorted. "I can tell you right now, it is not. I'm not going to have you use your personal assassin at the slightest provocation. Jerod belongs in *jail*. There's a massive difference between him and Connor."

"Okay, okay," I said, raising my hands in surrender. "Your choice. But I just wanted to let you know the option is there. Also, if I get my hands on him first, I can't promise what I will or won't do."

"Don't get yourself arrested for murder over someone like him," Jake warned.

"Someone who shot you? That's exactly the kind of person I would get myself arrested over."

"He shot me in the butt, not the chest."

I grinned. "Yeah, he did."

Jake rolled his eyes. "You're really never going to let me live that down, are you?"

"Of course not. You got shot in the butt, and it's hilarious. But also, it's going to be much less funny if you die, so now it's time for you to rest. Take the few days in the hospital. Recover from your surgery. I'm safe. Connor Ham is dead. And I'm going to find Jerod and bring him to justice— which means arrested, not dead."

Jake smiled. "You know, I never thought I'd be relieved to hear that you were just going to hunt down a person who shot me. But given what you've gone through, I know you can handle it. And I know nothing I can do or say will stop you. So, okay, you have my blessing. Go and find Jerod. But be careful."

"I always am."

"I don't believe a single word of that sentence."

God, I loved that man. I flashed him a grin. "Oh, and you know how you said my nicknames sucked? I finally found the perfect one."

Jake groaned and grabbed the pillow, shoving it over his face. "All right, let me have it."

"Jessica Flasher."

I cackled and jumped out of the way as Jake threw the pillow at me.

BOOK 10 - VOLCANO VIOLENCE: WITH JAKE ON the mend, Charlie decides she's going to hunt down the man who shot him and bring him to justice. But that soon turns out to be harder than Charlie expects, with the man in question having fled to the Big Island.

Away from her home base and the island she knows and loves, Charlie finds herself facing new challenges, but also getting new business as well. As it turns out, the Big Island is full of its own shady characters, and Charlie is hired to bring one of them to justice.

But as she gets closer to finding the man who shot Jake, Charlie realizes he's going to stop at nothing to keep his freedom. Even if that means getting rid of Charlie.

Click or tap here to pre-order your copy of Volcano Violence now.

About the Author

Jasmine Webb is a thirty-something who lives in the mountains most of the year, dreaming of the beach. When she's not writing stories you can find her chasing her old dog around, hiking up moderately-sized hills, or playing Pokemon Go.

Sign up for Jasmine's newsletter to be the first to find out about new releases here: http://www.authorjasminewebb.com/newsletter

You'll also receive the short story describing how Dot and Rosie met.

You can also connect with her on other social media:

Also by Jasmine Webb

Charlotte Gibson Mysteries

Aloha Alibi

Maui Murder

Beachside Bullet

Pina Colada Poison

Hibiscus Homicide

Kalikimaka Killer

Surfboard Stabbing

Mai Tai Massacre

Turtle Terror

Volcano Violence (coming March 2024)

Poppy Perkins Mysteries

Booked for Murder

Read Between the Lies

On the Slayed Page

Put Pen to Perpetrator

Turn Over a New Lead (coming December 2023)

Mackenzie Owens Mysteries

Dead to Rights

Against the Odds

Blast from the Past (coming January 2024)

Made in the USA
Las Vegas, NV
07 January 2024

84026609R00184